SHE GOT WHAT SHE WANTED
by Orrie Hitt

Black Gat Books • Eureka California

SHE GOT WHAT SHE WANTED

Published by Black Gat Books
A division of Stark House Press
1315 H Street
Eureka, CA 95501, USA
griffinskye3@sbcglobal.net
www.starkhousepress.com

ISBN: 978-1-944520-04-5

Book design by Mark Shepard, SHEPGRAPHICS.COM
Cover art by Joshua Rutherford

First Black Gat Edition: August 2016

FIRST EDITION

Also from Stark House Press by Orrie Hitt:
The Cheaters / Dial "M" for Man

I

The hot July sun bore down through the early morning fog and quickly lost some of its brilliance as it slammed up against the weatherbeaten clapboards of the Banners' home. The six-room frame house had been in the Banners family for over a hundred years—and on the books of various building-and-loans during most of that period. It clung there to the sprawling mud bank above the narrow brook, its porches sagging.

Every other windstorm some of the loose bricks fell off the top of the chimney and landed with a loud splash in the water below. There wasn't much of the chimney left any more. There wasn't a hell of a lot of house left, either.

Della Banners lay in her bed in an upstairs bedroom, yawning sleepily, breathing deep of the fresh, clean air that poured in through the open window.

"Holy Peter!" she said, opening her eyes wide and staring at the window.

There wasn't any glass in the bottom sash; a falling icicle, late the previous spring, had knocked both of the panes out. Her father had not replaced them, saying that having them out would save a lot of lost motion during the summer, putting the window up and down, but he added that he would get around to fixing it before winter. She believed him—maybe he'd nail a board over it, or something like that—because Chuck Banners hated cutting firewood worse than he hated going to church. And he seldom went to church, only to a funeral once in a while. He never did anything, except a little breathing and a lot of drinking. Most likely he'd never fix the window at all; just cut the heat off from her room and tell Della that she could undress and dress in the bathroom. Well, she didn't give a simple damn what he planned to tell her. She wouldn't be around to listen to it.

Critically, Della's blue-gray eyes surveyed the room. She saw where the paper hung away from the ceiling in one corner, brown and dry. This had been caused by one of the numerous leaks in the roof. There was the old oak sideboard which her father still maintained was a dresser, which his mother used to own. There was the ancient Morris chair with a broken back and with one leg shorter than the rest.

In growing disgust, Della looked at the new pink curtains which she had hung at the window only two weeks before. They had looked so pretty in the store, warm and soft; now they looked like everything else in the room. They didn't look like anything anybody would want to bother owning.

Della closed her eyes and shuddered. What a goat's nest, she thought. Ever since she could remember she had slept in this room, and every morning during her almost twenty years had been the same. Except this one. Somehow, this morning seemed to be different.

With the slow grace of a creeping cat she threw off the sheet and got out of bed. Her legs flashed white and straight and smooth in the slanting rays of the sun. Confidently, she went and stood before the mirror that rested at an angle on top of the sideboard. With slow deliberation she took a physical inventory of all the assets she possessed. She didn't miss a thing. There wasn't a thread of clothes on her body.

Her legs were long and firm, rounding out at the calves, swelling in slow easy curves until they reached her full thighs. At this point she turned sideways in order to get a better view. Her hips were white and round and solid. Her stomach, in sharp contrast, was slim and flat, pulling in just a little at the navel. The small of her back arched sharply above her buttocks. When her eyes caught the outline of her breasts in the mirror, she paused and smiled. They were full and round, the nipples dark and red, pointing forward and upward like twin roses on a vine. Some day, she supposed, she would have to buy a brassiere. Maybe when she got older, and after she had her first baby. She shuddered again. What awful thoughts so early in the morning!

Next, she looked at her face. And now she was confused, just as she was always confused when she stared back at those blue-gray eyes. They never seemed to be the same color. At times they were steady, unforgiving, and at other times, completely passionate and abandoned of all things moral. But, she thought, they went well with the rest of her face, and she was glad of that.

Her hair was blonde, naturally so and not with the aid of any rinse. Her nose was small, slightly upturned, yet absolutely adequate. Her lips were full and soft, generally moist, always sensual despite any lack of make-up. Her chin was round and smooth, blending precisely with the sleek lines of her throat, and the wide, deep hollow between her breasts.

She turned away from the mirror. She had seen enough. And then she laughed. She had just looked at some of the things that a lot of men had desired, few had attained, and no man had ever kept.

Just at that moment a car came up the bumpy lane which extended from Dingle Daisy Road, across the brook, wandered off to one side of the house, and ended in a tangle of briars and old wagon wheels.

Without looking out of the window, Della knew that this was not a neighbor's car, since she could hear no squeak of weakened springs crying out at the chug holes. She heard the car stop and a horn blow loud and long. Shambles, the Banners' big brown and white dog of doubtful ancestry, started barking from where he was chained at one end of the chicken coop.

Della heard the slam of the front screen door and her mother's familiar voice demand of the world in general: "Godammit, shut up!"

The dog stopped barking and the driver of the car took his arm off the horn.

"Whatta you want?" Della's mother asked sullenly.

"Oh, just making my monthly trip," a man's deep voice answered.

"Yeah?"

Della picked up her robe from the end of her bed and shrugged into it. Then she went over and stood near the side of the window. She looked through the mesh curtains, across the curled wood shingles on the porch roof, and down into the yard.

"I'm from the finance company," the man said.

The man was of medium height, heavy-set, and he had an enormous red face. His shirt was open at the throat and the sleeves were rolled up part way over huge forearms. He stood in front of a new Kaiser, one hand on the red hood and the other hand brushing at the deer flies that buzzed around his head.

"Which one?" Della's mother wanted to know.

"Is there more than one finance company?"

"Must be," her mother said. "Seems like there's a lot of different men coming around here all the time, saying they're from some finance company. But I don't pay any attention to them, Mister. I tell all of them, just like I'm telling you, the only way to settle these things is to see Mr. Banners."

"Would that settle it?" the man wanted to know, acidly.

"That ain't my business."

"Well," the man said. He shook his big head and pushed a hand through damp black hair. He looked up at the sun and blinked rapidly. "Where would I be apt to find Mr. Banners?"

Della's mother laughed. "I don't know, Mister. I've been

lookin' for Chuck myself, last day or so. I'm gettin' goddam sick of doin' his work."

The man stared around at the boards lying on the ground, the rusted sink by the side of the lane.

"Don't look like anybody's doing a hell of a lot," he observed.

"I'm gettin' sick of it, all the same," Della's mother insisted.

Della had heard her mother go through this same routine so many times that she felt like screaming. With a mounting feeling of disgust she stepped back from the window, untied the robe and flung it on the bed. She picked up a green organdy dress from the back of a chair, thought only briefly about wearing a slip, and then with a vicious tug brought the dress down over her body.

Probably her father was sitting out there in the barn at this very moment, debating with himself how he could best swing another deal and swindle somebody else out of the necessary funds to get his present creditors temporarily out of his life.

Della went back to the window.

"Mrs. Banners," the man said, suddenly, "this husband of yours is some character!"

"I don't deny it."

For a long moment the man stared in the direction of the porch.

"He ain't the only one," the man stated flatly. "I've been here before, lady. I've been here so often I can almost call this place home. And you know it."

Della's mother made no comment.

"I wish you people had something of value around here," the man said. "Maybe I could grab enough stuff to satisfy the company's loan." The collector sighed and shook his head. "I'd get it out of here, even if I had to carry it on my back."

"Well," came Mrs. Banners' sharp retort, "help yourself.

None of it's nailed down."

"Or would hold a nail," the man rejoined bitterly. He was silent for a long moment. Then, as he looked around the area again, his voice floated up to Della, this time urgent and excited. "Hey, lady! How about that car over there? Yours, ain't it? Sure is. Don't lie to me about it! How come I never saw that before? That's okay, lady? A Buick, too, and no later than a forty-one. Say, now!"

Della jammed her feet into her shoes and pulled back the curtains. She saw that the man had left his car and was now walking quickly toward the black club coupe parked almost out of sight behind the dilapidated smoke-house.

"You leave that car alone!" Della shouted after him. "That car belongs to me!"

The man stopped and turned around slowly. He opened his mouth to express his views on the matter, took another good look at Della's blonde head framed in the window, then clamped his jaw shut. A couple of frantic flies showed up silver in the sun as they buzzed around his head. He took a couple of slow steps toward the house, looked up at her more closely, and swung one big hand aimlessly at the flies.

"Well, now," he repeated.

"That car belongs to me," Della told him again. Her voice was low and gentle. She smiled and the big man glanced down at the ground and kicked a stone out of the way with a polished shoe.

"Lady," he said, "if that's your car I wouldn't touch it with a ten foot pole." He glanced up again and leered as he saw how her dress fell away at the top. "Matter of fact, I wouldn't touch anything you've got."

Della looked down at him disinterestedly.

"Don't let it worry you," she told him shortly. "You won't get the chance."

She wheeled from the window, raced through the bedroom and into the hall. The heels of her shoes rapped hard on the unpainted boards as she clattered down the stairs. She pushed open the screen door and went out onto the porch; the screen door stood open, not closing by itself, because someone had broken the spring a couple of summers before, and it hadn't been repaired.

Her mother, who was standing by the porch railing, looked at Della briefly. No emotion showed on Mrs. Banners' thin, expressionless face. The faded blue wash dress which she wore and which had changed hands countless times during various rummage sales, clung to her as though it were a burlap bag.

Mrs. Banners was a woman of small stature, her shoulders rounded from a lifetime of trying—and failing. She was, Della thought, a woman who had lost all the ambitions of her earlier life, if she'd ever had any. Ever since Della could remember, her mother hadn't seemed to care about herself, or the appearance of the house, or anything. Mrs. Banners just got up in the morning and went through the day and went to bed at night. There wasn't, Della thought, much more to it than that.

"Good morning, Mother," Della said, cheerfully.

Her mother stared back at her, just as she always did. "What's all the fuss?" Della asked.

Her mother shrugged. "You ought to know as much 'bout it as I do. You been listenin' just like you always listen. That's why you wanted the front room, so's you wouldn't miss nothin'."

"She ain't missing anything," the man said. By this time he had walked back to the porch. He stood at the bottom of the steps, looking up at Della and grinning. Something in his eyes told Della that she might just as well be standing there naked. She guessed that the light behind her revealed the fact that she wasn't wearing any slip. She wondered if he could tell that she wasn't wearing any panties, either. She went over and stood against the side of the house.

"Why ain't you working this morning?" Della's mother wanted to know.

"It's Sunday."

"Huh!"

"Well, it's Sunday. I never work on Sunday."

"Who said you did?" Her mother looked down at her hands which were stained brown from pulling the weeds out of the garden they had in a rock pile in back of the house. "Where in Heaven's name does the time go to?"

That didn't seem to call for any comment.

"If it's Sunday, what're you doing here?" her mother asked the big man.

The man's eyes moved away from the points of Della's breasts and became sullen as he regarded Mrs. Banners again.

"Company punishment, that's what it is. The boss made me come out here on Sunday, this time, just to impress on me what a fool I was to loan any money to that no-good husband of yours." The big man glanced around helplessly. "I sure wish that I could find him."

"I don't know where he is," Mrs. Banners said again. "I wished I did. I'm gettin' mighty sick of doing all his—"

"My name's Carter," the man said, suddenly ignoring Mrs. Banners and staring back at Della. He lowered one eyelid and laughed. "John Carter."

Della didn't say anything.

"Maybe you could help me, Miss?" he suggested, trying another approach. "I'll bet you know where I can find your daddy."

Mrs. Banners' voice was sharp.

"She don't know nothin'," she said, glaring at Della.

The hot sun poured onto the porch, burned through Della's thin dress and stung at her flesh. She was sick of the whole thing, completely so. In the shimmering heat waves she could see the faces of the countless men who had, over the years, come looking for Chuck Banners.

And she could hear her father talking to them, getting out of one fix right into another. She could also hear her father discussing numerous propositions with her mother over coffee and cigarettes—he generally needed his wife's signature on some kind of paper or other—and she knew that her mother never listened very much, or cared. Her mother always signed her name. Like the time Chuck had put a chattel on the pony which an uncle, now dead, had given to Della one Christmas. Chuck had wound up on the short end of that note, and the horse had been taken away, although Chuck had told Della that it was just as well because it was sure a lot of bother cutting hay for it.

She hadn't felt that way about it at all, and she had cried a long time about it. Her father had listened to that for a couple of days, and then he'd gone out and brought home a dog for her. The dog had been a German Shepherd, and smart, but she'd only had him a few weeks when her father was arrested for stealing the dog, and the big, shaggy animal had been returned to his rightful owner.

It made Della sick just thinking about his deals. Of course, some of them had worked, like the one about the car. That deal had worked—to Della's advantage.

"Sure, I know where my father is," Della said.

The man grinned.

"I always say, you've got to ask an honest person to get an honest answer. 'Course, Mrs. Banners, with all apologies to you, that don't mean—"

"You shut your big mouth!" Mrs. Banners told Della, nervously wiping her hands on the sides of her dress.

The man started to climb up to the porch, but the steps groaned loudly under his weight and he jumped back again.

"I ain't no cop," he said. "Lord, no! I'm just a guy who trusts people and who can't make a living doing it. I just want to talk to—ah, Chuck. You know, figure this thing out so he can do what's right. Cripes, lady—"

"He's probably out in the barn," Della said. "You can find him there."

She stopped talking and ducked under her mother's swinging arm. Mrs. Banners grabbed hold of a porch post to keep from falling down the steps. The man jumped back out of the way, his eyes never lifting from the dark hollow at the top of Della's dress.

"That's a dirty lie!" Mrs. Banners shouted.

Mr. Carter turned, looked around and started walking toward the rickety barn.

"You come back here!"

Mr. Carter kept right on walking. He went around the corner of the house, whistling.

"You dog!" Mrs. Banners flung at Della as she went down the steps and hurried after Mr. Carter.

Della smiled. She patted her hair and stared thoughtfully at the Buick coupe. It had a nice black finish and it was clean inside. The white rims Della had bought for the wheels made it look pretty good. Good enough to sell for a fairly decent price. And it hadn't cost her a nickel.

She recalled the day during the past winter when her father had driven it home. At first she had wondered how he could afford to buy such a late model car—indeed, any kind of a car at all—but that night at supper he had patiently explained the intricate financial transactions which preceded the purchase.

Through the farm bureau he had managed to get a small amount of money for the purpose of improving some of his land, posting a second mortgage as security. This amount had been used to pay off the chattel mortgage which had been on the household furniture. As soon as he had done that he had gone to another finance company and re-borrowed a much larger sum on the furniture. This company had not had any previous experience with Chuck and he had handed them a rather imposing list of holdings. Since there had been about two feet of snow on the ground at the time—a factor which Chuck had counted upon heavily —there had been no appraisal of the furniture and the loan had been granted.

A few days after that, Della's father had purchased the car, making a substantial down payment with his borrowed capital and financing the balance due.

This arrangement, Della remembered, had stood up under more or less constant pressure for about two months. Then the payments became too frequent and large—five dollars for just one time would have fit into that category—and once again Chuck Banners was faced with financial disaster. At this point, and reluctantly, he had appealed to Della for help.

Although she hadn't been able to save anything from her small wages, which she earned typing in Layton's office, Della had agreed to do what she could. On one condition. That the car be signed over to her. In a rare moment of complete despair her father had reluctantly agreed. Della had immediately arranged to borrow the necessary funds—with no idea of ever paying it back, of course—from one Lincoln Rodney, who was married, had a wife and two children, and who had been her English teacher during her last year in high school.

Rodney hadn't wanted to part with the money—he'd said there were Easter outfits to buy for the family, and a lot of stuff like that. But he'd given it to her. It hadn't been necessary for Della to remind him that he had taught her more than English that last year, in the projection booth up in the balcony of the school auditorium. She'd guessed, as he'd handed her the roll of bills, that he was just a little bit sorry about it.

Della's thoughts were interrupted by the return of her mother, the perspiring finance company collector, and a slim man of good height who had an unconcerned grin on his face and a jaunty lilt to his walk.

"There's no use gettin' excited about this," Della heard

her father say. "No use to it at all. There's an old saying that you can't get blood out of a stone—"

"Or money out of a Banners," Carter injected.

Chuck Banners laughed. Della's heart twisted and stabbed at her in pain. Really, he was such a nice person. Why, he didn't look forty-five years old. True, his hair was gray, but he wasn't bald and it was always neatly trimmed and well combed. His face was rugged and firm, almost bronze in color. Sometimes he went fishing down by the brook, but he seldom worked very hard at it, just lay there on the bank looking up into the sky. His shoulders were square, broad for his five foot ten, and the plaid shirts he always wore gave him an outdoorsy look. At the present time he was wearing the familiar dungarees, rolled up high, almost above his ankles, not unlike some high school kid.

All of them came up onto the porch and gathered around Della. The porch sills groaned under their weight. Carter didn't seem alarmed, being more intent upon the little mole that Della had at the hollow of her throat. Mrs. Banners leaned over, grabbed a handful of skirt and mopped the sweat from her forehead.

"I've got a deal on," Della's father announced, nodding at his daughter. "I been telling this fellow here about this car of yours. I tell him it's all paid for and that—well, maybe, tomorrow morning you could raise some cash on it. Maybe old Layton would loan it to you."

The way old Layton had taken to looking her over at the office, he'd probably give Della almost anything—if he knew he was going to get what he wanted in return.

"No," Della said, emphatically.

"I'll pay you back," Chuck said.

Della shook her head.

"Besides, I haven't got any job," Della said. Her mother stopped wiping her forehead and her father almost stopped breathing; Della's money had bought the food and paid the taxes since she'd got out of school. "Mr. Layton closed his law office. Yesterday. That was my last day."

"The bastard!" Chuck Banners said, looking at Carter as though he were seeking some kind of confirmation of the description he had just given the senior lawyer in Hurley.

"I hear he's going to get married," Carter said. "To that Winnie dame. The one with the kid."

"Both the Winnie girls have kids," Chuck said.

"It's the one that ain't already married," Carter said. "Her name's Flossie. I've heard that it's his kid she's got. I don't know. It don't seem right. Why, he's old enough to be resurrected."

Seventy, Della thought. Layton's body was seventy, but his eyes hadn't gone past his thirty-fifth birthday. She knew. Those eyes had been on her constantly for the year and a half that she'd worked for him. All over her. And she could still smell that awful garlic on his breath. She felt sorry for Flossie. Flossie had been a nice kid, smart with the books in school but awful dumb with the boys after school hours.

"You ought to help me out," Chuck said, addressing Della again. "If I can just get this settled, why—"

Della smiled at him sweetly. Mr. Carter gave her a broad grin and her father frowned. Her mother walked to the screen door and paused.

"I'm not borrowing on the car," Della said. "So you won't have to worry about paying me back."

"That's right," Chuck Banners shouted angrily. "Dammit, kick me when I'm down!"

Della walked past her mother and on into the house.

"You should look for another job," Della's mother said, hopefully. "Next month is taxes, you know. You could get up early in the morning, Della, and—"

"I'm already up," Della said from the stairs. "Now. I'm going today."

She went up to her room and took an old suitcase out from under her bed, the suitcase which she had used for her graduation trip to Washington. Its black imitation leather was ripped in a few places and there was a large spot of mildew on one side. She tried to rub the grayish scum off with a kleenex, but quickly gave that up. What the hell, she could get a new one in a day or so.

It didn't take her long to put her clothes inside the suitcase. When she had finished she stood there looking contemptuously at the faded blues and reds, the three pairs of stockings with runs in them and the extra pair of shoes with the leather chipped off the heels. Quickly she retrieved a slip from the suitcase, took off the dress she was wearing, put on the slip, then got into the dress again. As an afterthought she found a pair of step-ins—they had Saturday printed on one side of them and had been special at three for two dollars from a mail order house.

With sharp finality she closed the suitcase, tried a couple of times to get the snaps to come together, gave up in disgust, and tossed the thing back under the bed.

She walked out of the room without bothering to look back. There wasn't a damn thing there that she wanted to see again.

2

As Della reached the bottom of the stairs she heard her father and mother and the finance company man talking in the kitchen.

"Here's to it!" her father laughed. "Better luck next time!"

"Yeah!" Carter agreed, and then he, too, laughed.

Della decided that her father must have located a jug of whiskey some place. Along about dark the fat finance company man would leave the Banners home with his pockets full of promises and his head spinning like a kid's top. Following this the Banners would start to fight and the noise would only terminate much later, when they climbed into bed and the springs started to creak. There, struggling in the torn sheets, they would momentarily forget their differences.

"So long!" Della shouted.

There was silence from the kitchen, and no one bothered answering her. She kicked the screen door open and went out.

She went down the lane, keeping to the edge and walking in the grass so that she wouldn't have to feel the round stones on her feet.

The Buick was parked alongside the smoke-house, in the shade of a butternut tree. She got in and rolled the windows down, reached up one long leg and kicked the ventilator open. Then she got the key out of the glove compartment, put it in the switch, and started the car. She glanced at the gas gauge and saw that there was barely a quarter of a tank.

"Damn!" she said.

Then she thought of Roy Donaldson and the gasoline station which he had just bought near Hurley, six miles away. She smiled and let the clutch out. She didn't have to worry about gas.

She drove down the lane and the big car took the chug holes slow and easy like. It was a good car, not bad looking, and it had plenty of wallop on the road. She was sorry that she'd have to sell it. Then she remembered that it hadn't cost her anything and she didn't feel so badly. It was funny, she thought, but she had paid for that car during her last year in high school. She hadn't really known about it then, of course, because at the time she had been anxious only to get a passing mark in English. She'd been doing good work in her tests and all that, but she'd seldom had a chance to do any work in class. Rodney hadn't called on her, just looked at her whenever she crossed her legs or smiled, and then looked away again.

In May of that year he was still looking at her like that, then away again, and her report cards were just as bad as ever. She decided to see him after school and talk to him about it, but when she went to his room there was a lot of other kids there, and he just told her that she ought to hurry or she'd miss the bus.

The next afternoon, when she'd seen him go into the projection room in the balcony, she'd waited a couple of minutes and followed him. The pin at the top of her dress had broken, revealing the sharp deep line between her breasts. She'd found him in the booth, fooling with some film, and he hadn't known she was there until her hand touched his arm.

"Mr. Rodney," Della had said, "I wanted to talk to you about my marks."

He hadn't said anything, just stood there looking at her in the half light. She'd felt her breasts rising and falling, and she'd known that his eyes were fastened down there, watching them.

"I want to pass," she'd said. "So much!"

And she had. She didn't want to put up with another year of school, wearing the same clothes, having the guys and the girls always laughing at how she looked—the guys a little sore because she stayed strictly away from them, and the girls hoping she would continue wearing the same sloppy rags because it was the only way that they, as still growing girls, could compete with Della's thirty-four hips, twenty-three waist, and thirty-seven bust that didn't need a brassiere.

"You'll pass," Mr. Rodney said, his voice a little hoarse.

"But my marks—"

They hadn't done any talking about her marks. He'd put a hand down there, cupping one of her breasts, hurting her and making her cry just a little. Then he'd reached over and slammed the projection room door shut with his other hand, pushing his body close to her.

"Wow!" he kept saying. "Wow!"

She'd known what he was going to do, and she'd been afraid, but she hadn't been able to stop him.

"Don't tear my dress," she'd pleaded with him.

He'd kissed her hard and long, bruising her mouth, pushing his tongue in there between her lips.

"Damn you!" he'd said. "You've been driving me crazy!"

He'd torn her dress in several places, trying to get it out of the way after he'd thrown her down on top of a carton of films. His fingers had dug deep into her flesh, and he had hurt her a lot.

Later, he'd stood near the door of the booth, barring her way, his long frame shaking.

"I didn't know," he kept saying over and over, and she could tell that he was crying. "Della, I didn't know. I thought—"

She got to her feet, her legs aching. Straightening out her dress, she had seen the long tear down the front but she had been too numb to cry about it.

"Please take me home," was all she'd said.

And he'd driven her home that night, not saying a word, and he'd cried all the way there. When he'd let her out at the entrance of the lane, she'd stood there by the side of the car for just a moment. He hadn't looked at her or said anything.

"After that," she'd told him, turning away, "I'd better pass."

Della had been in the top ten of her class.

Mr. Rodney hadn't looked at her after that, until the night she'd hit him up for the money to sink into this car. He'd looked at her plenty then. And he'd told her about the kids, and their Easter clothes, and how his wife wasn't well and yelling at him all the time. That sure is tough, she thought. The poor, stupid jerk!

She drove off the lane and turned right onto the yellow dirt road that skirted the Willowkill all the way to Harris. A short distance down the road she had to stop while some kids in shorts, guarded like jailbirds by a couple of college kids also in shorts, crossed the road and moved off through a field. The kids, she knew, were from one of the boys' camps up in the mountains, out for their daily hike.

Farther down the road she encountered several couples, from nearby boarding houses, strolling alongside the road. They were on both sides of the road, making it almost impossible to pass. She put her hand on the horn, but the only response to that was one of the fat ladies turning her head and smiling stupidly.

She pushed the car between them.

"Why don'tcha look where you're goin'?" one of the men snarled, whacking at one of the tires with a stick.

She drove on down the road, burning inside. That was just one of the things she hated about this damned country. It was the same thing every summer, hundreds of people coming up from the city and wandering all over the place as if they had a first mortgage on everything. There were the kids' camps, both boys and girls, with the wise guys from the colleges who came up to be counselors, and the coy girls who came up to be with the boys. Some of the fellows were all right, though. Like that fellow Ike—what was his last name?—who had been over at Timberhead Camp a couple of summers before. That was the year Della had gotten fifty per month and tips for hopping tables at the Wellington Hotel.

She'd met Ike one night at the pool—he'd had a friend staying at the hotel—and they'd gone swimming every night for a week after that. She'd liked him, his quick wit, his long brown body and his rather long blond hair. She'd liked him until one of the other waitresses told her that he had a boy friend and that's why he hung around the hotel so much. It had made Della a little sick.

She slowed up as she went by the Jennings farm, noticing the weeds that grew high around the small, gray-shingled house, the hay rake that stood rusty and unused in the jungle of briars that had at one time been a fine raspberry patch. She saw Mrs. Jennings' slight form on the porch, rocking in her chair in her customary white dress. She waved, but Mrs. Jennings didn't wave back. She guessed that Mrs. Jennings was thinking of her son who had been in Korea and who had died there.

The dirt road broke out onto macadam as she crossed the county line. The road wasn't very good, but it wasn't dusty and from here on into Hurley the hotels were bigger and closer together. She drove by these, the tennis courts and the swimming pools and the long shaded porches that were crawling with people. Tonight, being Sunday, many of the men would have to return to the city, leaving their families until the following Friday night. Most of the women who had kids, and those who didn't have kids, would get along all right and be happy until about the coming Wednesday night. By that time they'd just about be out of the money which their husbands had left, and they'd still want to do things. And they'd do them.

They'd do plenty with the local yokels who had dance permits at the hotels and who came out not to dance but to see how long it took to get into another guy's bed. These were the same guys who couldn't find a lick of work in the winter, unless they were lucky and somebody gave them a contract cutting cordwood, or getting out poles. Some of these guys went to Florida, following the hotel crowd, writing smart letters back home, sending dirty cards to the girls around town, and coming back in the spring with their pocketbooks as flat as last year's plowed ground.

At the four corners Della had to stop and wait for the

church crowd to get squared off and into their cars. One thing about the Catholics, she thought, you had to hand it to them. They could build a church up in the sticks, like this one, and fill it every Sunday. There was a Protestant church on the opposite corner but that had been closed for a number of years. The windows were now boarded up, this having been done a few years back when it was discovered that the place of worship was being used by some of the Lexington Avenue girls who came up, seven to a car, for a weekend of play with the boys and their cash. Now the girls stayed in the hotels, or hired taxi cabs, or just went off back of the tennis courts.

The road leveled out and the fields got wider and greener and the farms looked better. The hotels along the road were bigger now, and the cars in front of them were bigger, too. The people got to the side of the road when she blew the horn. This was the smart crowd and their faces were sharper, the women slimmer than those at the hotels further up the Willowkill.

She drove slowly past the Wellington Hotel, its cream-colored stucco rising high into the blue sky, sticking out like a big box against the background of dark green hills. No one was out on the tennis court—the clay got very hot at midday—but the pool was full and there was a big dopey crowd relaxing on the front porch. A guy in white was out near the old barn that had been converted into quarters for the waitresses. She supposed that he was dumping garbage, smelling up the place just like always. She'd spent that one summer living there, and she remembered how hot it had been at night, and the bats that got inside, and the girl down at the end who cried all the time, because she'd got caught and the guy had checked out.

That had been the summer before Roy went away, the year he had quit college because his father was so sick. Roy had come up to see her every night, smelling of clean hay, his face cool and smooth from the shaving lotion that he used. For a while, she had thought that she was in love with Roy. She had basked in the delight of this until the night he'd told her that he had a job in Arabia, that he would be gone for two years, that he loved her and that he wanted her to wait for him. He'd told her how much he was going to make, how much he could save even with his father being sick, what his plans were when he got back.

She turned left at the bridge, glancing only briefly down at the wide bridle path where she had parked with Roy that night, where he'd told her that he loved her—and where they'd stayed until the fog of morning was thick over the water and he was satisfied.

After that night she had been convinced of only one thing: Roy was like all the rest, like Mr. Rodney, like a hound dog that had broken his leash. Because Roy hadn't called on the phone or seen her before going away, and now he'd been back home for over a month and she hadn't heard from him.

Well, she thought, turning in at the gas station, it should have been worth ten gallons of gas. That's only a little over two dollars and the girls from Lexington Avenue got from twenty to a hundred for the night. And they never loved the man. Della had.

Roy came out, even before she stopped the car. He went around to the back of the car and she could hear him take off the gas cap. He turned on the pump, came up alongside of the car and slapped a sponge against the dusty windshield.

"How many?"

She didn't say anything, just sat there smiling. He stopped rubbing on the glass and bent down, looking inside. His face was almost copper in color, his hair shining black and inclined to be curly. He had a long, firm nose and dark eyes that set deep in his face.

"Della!"

"How are you, Roy?"

He looked at the sponge, squeezing it until the water dripped out.

"Okay."

She pushed at her hair and gave him the kind of a smile that she knew he liked.

"I was going to call you," he said. He rubbed his lower teeth against his upper lip. "I don't know why I didn't."

"We don't have a phone any more."

"I guess I know," he said.

"I heard you bought the gas station. I typed up the papers."

"Oh. You must have been out to lunch the day I signed them."

"I guess I was."

The silence hung in the heat.

"Business is pretty good," he said.

"I didn't want any gas," she told him. "Just saying hello."

He glanced at the humming pump, then jumped toward the hose. She leaned over and looked out. The gas had run down the fender and onto the ground.

"Well, that's all right," Roy said, wiping the fender with a rag. "Don't worry about it."

"I'll pay you tomorrow," she said.

He kept on wiping at the fender.

"I'll stop by and pay you tomorrow," she told him again.

He threw the cloth down onto the ground and screwed the gas cap on. His face was hard and strained as he came back and stood leaning up against the car door.

"Dammit," he said, "I'm not worrying about the gas." He thrust his head inside, up close to her, his dark eyes staring at her full red lips. "Jeez!" he said.

Inside the gas station the telephone was ringing, but he

didn't pay any attention to it. A couple of cars went by, one of them loaded on top with beds and springs and mattresses. Pretty soon the phone stopped ringing.

"Della," he said, his face tightening at her smile. "Della, won't you understand something?"

Down inside she laughed at him.

"Sure," she said. "You don't want me to pay for the gas."

"It isn't that. You know it isn't that." He looked away from her, down the road, at the point where the guy had stopped and was putting some more rope around the beds and junk on top of his car. "It's about that night. You know the one."

"There were a lot of nights, Roy," she reminded him.

"I'm talking about that last night."

"Oh."

"Well, Della, I thought about that night for two years. Honest I did! Out there in the desert, where your razor gets so hot you could burn your face with it, where the only thing you ever see is an Arab. Damn the Arabs! You could smell them hours before you saw them. And when one of them gets punished for a crime, they cut off his right hand so that he can't—" He looked back at her again, leaning further into the car, his face much closer. "I wanted to write, Della. Honest. I did write, a lot of letters."

"I never got them."

"That's because I tore them up. I couldn't say what I wanted to say. It was about that night. I was mixed up— I was going away, and I felt sorry for myself, and I hated every minute of the waiting. Then we parked down there by the stream, and I knew I was leaving you and when I kissed you, everything just let go."

He stopped talking, and she could tell from his eyes that he was back there along that bank, with the fog thick and close around them again, just their bodies and the night knowing that time was endless.

"It's all right," Della said quietly. "You don't have to apologize."

"You're not sore?"

"Of course not."

"I—I thought—"

"You thought wrong," she said, her voice gentle.

A couple of more cars went by, the big cars from the classy hotels, hurtling carelessly down the road.

"There was so much I wanted that summer," he said. "Until that Arabia job came along, I was sort of mixed up, I guess. I wanted father to get well, but—"

"I'm sorry about him," Della said.

Roy swallowed hard. "They tell me—there wasn't much left of him."

Della thought briefly of the shriveled form that had lain in the casket in the big, flower-smelling room of Hector and Robbins.

"Yes," she said, almost shuddering.

"Some day they'll find out," he said. "They won't do it with dimes or knocking on people's doors and begging for money. Some day, maybe, we'll get a government that thinks as much of spending money to save people's lives as it does to figure out ways to destroy them."

Della hoped that Roy wasn't going to take off on that angle again. It was funny that she had forgotten about the things he had talked of almost constantly that last summer. He'd been critical of the town Board of Health that never inspected anything except the quality of the liquor in the local taverns, of the assessors who couldn't tell the difference between a fertile field and a stone quarry—of a million and one things that all hinged upon what other people didn't do right. She guessed that Roy ought to be in politics.

"I don't know just what I'll do with the place," she heard him saying. "Maybe I'll make a summer hotel out of it. It's big enough, and I could make a lake down there where the brook is narrow."

A fine hotel owner he'd make, she thought. The first guy who showed up with a dame and couldn't produce a marriage license would wind up in the clink.

"I guess you could," she said. She laughed, "If you didn't make out, you could always have a fire."

"They still do that?"

She shrugged and his eyes dropped with the movement of her dress.

"I'm glad you came by," he said, still looking down there. "I know you just don't pick up things after two years where you left them—but I'd like to try, Della."

She didn't lie to him. She just reached up one hand and patted his face.

"Maybe I can get away tomorrow night," he said, quickly. "I'm trying to get a kid to help me out and if he shows up tomorrow, why—"

Sure, she thought, maybe they could go up by the brook again. How nice. For Roy. Before that first time she had thought that he loved her, believed it. And then, after he'd got what he wanted, he hadn't said he loved her. He hadn't said anything. And now he was back again, still not saying it, but still wanting the same thing.

"I've been tied down," he said, laughing a little. "I've been in town twice in the last three weeks. Almost as bad as Arabia."

Della turned the switch on.

"Well," she said.

He hung there inside the car, trying to keep her.

"I suppose you're going into town."

"I'm going through town," she said.

"Maybe you'd do me a favor."

She turned the switch off.

"There's a slot at the First National Bank where you can drop money in," he said. "Right by the front door."

"Mr. Layton used to use it."

"Well, you know where it is, then." He stepped back from the car. "I'll only be a minute, Della. The slip's all made up. I was going to send it down with the mailman, first thing in the morning, but sometimes he doesn't like to take it. You wouldn't mind taking it, would you?"

"No," she said, "I'll take it."

He went around the front of the car and walked into the station. The hot sun poured through the windshield, dirty only where he had first wiped the sponge. The motor, cooling off now, cracked a couple of times. When he came back she had the motor running.

"I'm glad you came along," he said, handing her a greasy brown envelope.

She put the envelope on the seat beside her.

"So am I," she said.

"I'll get in touch with you tomorrow," he said.

Della nodded and put the car in gear. Some gravel slapped against the fenders and she drove to the highway and turned right. She had to slow up as a wagon piled high with hay crawled by; then she let the coupe wind itself up in second. She was doing fifty, sinking low into the cushions at the bumps, when she threw it into high.

She drove into Hurley, not slowing up too much, along the main street that was littered with Saturday night's beer cans and papers, past the diner where a drunk was lying on the sidewalk, surrounded by a bunch of laughing kids. When she got to the traffic light she stopped, waited for a big fat lady in shorts and halter to cross the street, then turned right onto Route 17.

The bank was on the left hand side, halfway down the block, just at the edge of where the business section stopped and the wide lawns and the big houses of the country club crowd began.

She just kept on going, pouring the gas to the Buick. To hell with stopping.

3

Della stood at the window of her hotel room, looking out into the gathering darkness. Below her, stretching away into the fog and rain, the neon-colored tangle of the city's lights came on, one at a time. From the nearby hills a train whistled, echoing sharp and long. She raised the window slowly and the acrid smell of coal smoke came out of the fog and into the room.

This was Della's third night in Port Keller. Actually, the city was not a port and it was not a city at all. Many years before it had been a port for the old D & H Canal, but the huge cut that had been built with the tears and the lives of men was now filled with garbage and ashes. Almost forty years previously Port Keller, after having attained ten thousand population, had been proclaimed a city. Now, it was around nine thousand, and it was still a city, and the mayor got his money every month, and the people griped because they were still paying city taxes. Della thought that the people didn't know how good they had it; they should live in Harris.

The first thing Della had done upon her arrival—or, at least, as early on Monday morning as possible—had been to sell the Buick for cash. After that she had made out a money order to Roy, explaining that she had forgotten to leave the money at the bank, and mailed his deposit back to him in a nice clean envelope. After that she'd purchased a few medium-priced dresses, a high-priced hairdo and paid a week's advance on a low-priced hotel room. Then she'd gone to the movies a couple of times, saw one picture over twice, still not getting her money's worth, dined in four different restaurants, including the hotel dining room, and fought off a magazine salesman who wanted to give her a subscription to something or other.

Right at the moment, Della was conscious of the need for some kind of employment. She was, she knew, a good typist, a fair bookkeeper, and an excellent looker. It seemed to be just a question as to which one of these accomplishments would take her the farthest in the shortest possible length of time.

Her skirt swirled as she turned away from the window. The new suntan dress clung to her full hips, pressed in snugly at the middle, flared out almost to overflowing at the top. The color emphasized the blonde richness of her hair, which the hairdresser had wanted to pile in a heap on top of her head. She was glad that she'd argued him out of it and that it now hung in a long wavy halo about her face.

She went to the lounge chair and flung herself into it. She kicked off her shoes, picked up a magazine and tried to read. Nothing seemed to interest her so she put the magazine down and picked up Port Keller's six page evening journalistic effort. She looked at the classified ads. The only ones listed in the female column were for women to sell things—Christmas cards at a huge profit, corsets that would put the worst figure in the best shape, and a new wonder pill called Keep-Me-Slim. She threw the paper down, got up and went over to the window again. She looked out, but this time she couldn't even get interested in the theater marquee.

Lord, she was lonely and bored stiff! Why hadn't she gone to New York, or some place like that? Even Binghamton. Or Albany. She'd heard a lot about Albany, about Hudson County. She glanced down at the street, at the gang of guys standing on the corner, and laughed. You didn't have to go to New York, or Albany, or any place like that, to sell that kind of stuff. You could sell that anywhere, if you were broke, or hard up, or just so stupid that you didn't know from nothing.

She crossed to the radio and turned it on. It wouldn't

play so she got a quarter out of her pocketbook and dropped it, grudgingly, into the slot. Just as some dance music came on, soft and low and lonesome, there was a knock at her door. She turned the radio volume down, went to the door and opened it.

"Not again!" she said.

All last night the guy next door had been fooling around her door. He'd been drunk, and the first time it'd been because he couldn't find his room. The other times he'd wandered out in the hall to her door, insisting that she should get out and give him a break.

"Oh!" Della said.

This man was big, not fat, young and with the finest proportioned facial features Della had ever seen. He stood there, filling the doorway, just looking at her.

"Why don't we double that?" he said, his voice clear and deep.

Della stared at the point where the red bow tie cut a V under his chin.

"A diamond for Jackson!"

"A—what?"

"A diamond. That's you. And Jackson. That's me."

He grinned broadly. His teeth were white and even, lighting up the dark tan of his face. He was conservatively dressed in a gray gaberdine suit, white shirt and the red bow tie that focused attention on his face. He wore no hat and his dark hair was tousled and unruly, as though it were accustomed to the sun and the wind and the rain.

"If you're selling riddles," Della told him, "you're knocking on the wrong door."

"I'm not selling anything," he said.

A siren wailed down in the street.

"Or buying," Della said, thinking of the looks and the double meaning words of the bellboy that first night. "It's still the wrong door."

"We'll find out about that."

He reached in his pocket and took out his wallet. He sorted out a bunch of cards, apparently did not find what he was looking for, then glanced through them again.

"Here it is," he said. He stared at the pink slip in his hand for an instant. "You're Della Banners, aren't you?"

"Yes."

"Then this is the right door. My name is Jackson, as I told you before. Jackson Bishop of the Wyandot Roofing Company." He chuckled and his eyes lighted up. "We also rebuild your sidewalls."

Her eyes found his face.

"There's nothing wrong with my roof," she said.

He looked her over thoroughly.

"Yeah, you've got a good roof," he said, nodding at her blonde head. Very deliberately he looked down at her legs, at her stockinged feet. "You've got a good foundation, too." His glance traveled along the lines of her body. "Nope, nothing wrong with your sidewalls, either."

Something strange crawled up her spine and spread over her shoulders. She stepped back, took a firm grip on the door and got ready to slam it.

"Listen, Miss Banners," he said, pushing his foot forward. "Before you rattle the hinges on that thing, will you sign—properly, this time—the transfer of ownership of your Buick coupe?"

She held fast to the doorknob.

"I sold the car. Monday."

"I know you did. And I bought it. Only now I find that you signed your name wrong. Look here. You see how it is on front? Della M. Banners. Now, see how you signed it on the back? Just Della Banners. The man at the Motor Vehicle Bureau told me to get you to sign it as you should, on the back. I guess the second-hand man didn't notice it, but that fellow in the clerk's office don't fool around."

"I guess I forgot."

"That's all right. I'm glad you did." When she didn't

give him the smile he was looking for, he asked, "What's the M stand for?"

He got his smile.

"Millicent."

She looked down at her toes, curling them, and swinging the door back and forth.

"Maybe, Miss Banners, if you would sign this again—" Her shoulders and back felt all right now, but there was a dull ache across the front of her dress.

"Sure," she said. "Come on in."

He didn't need a written invitation. He followed her over to the scratched desk and the door made a lot of noise closing by itself. He got out his pen and showed her where to sign the form. She wrote her name underneath where she had signed it before, gave him back his pen and they stood there looking at each other.

Jackson Bishop wasn't as big as he had seemed at first, but even with high heels Della wouldn't be much above his shoulders. There was a little scar along one side of his chin, cutting a thin white line through the brown of his skin. She wasn't quite sure just what color his eyes were, maybe hazel or brown, but she knew that he used them to advantage in his business because his feelings were in there, deep, and he kept stabbing away with them.

"You're truly beautiful," he told her finally.

Della knew that he'd been staring down the front of her dress as she'd bent over the desk. She decided that he was still trying to look the same place. She wondered why men did that. Why they seemed to use a woman's breasts as a yardstick for beauty. She could understand that with legs, because a man could see a lot of a girl's legs—all of her legs, if she wanted him to. It was just difficult to figure out why a man could look at a woman about a foot below her chin and decide that she was beautiful. He never knew if he was looking at the real thing or a couple of tennis balls.

"Leave me your address," she said acidly, "and I'll send you a quarter."

A little color flooded into his face, and he glanced away as she hauled up the front of her dress. He fumbled in his pocket, found a pack of Camels and handed her one.

"You're new in Port, aren't you?" he inquired as the smoke curled around them.

She nodded.

"You lived in Harris, then," he said, referring to the car registration.

"Too long."

"I used to fish up there. In the Willowkill. That's quite a while ago, though."

"That's all it's good for," she said.

"And you're new to Port?"

"You don't have to keep reminding me about it."

"I didn't mean it that way."

"Then stop saying it."

He thought about that for a minute.

She supposed that she should resent his questions, but she liked him, and the loneliness of a few minutes before was gone.

"Are you working?"

"Not yet, but I intend to start in a day or so."

"You've got a job?"

"Of course I've got a job!" she said, a little resentfully.

"What doing?"

"Well, I thought—"

He grinned and looked at his cigarette.

"Naturally you're lying about that,"

"Say, now—"

"Aren't you?"

Her eyes met his.

"You don't have to tell me," she said. "I know when I'm lying."

"But why do that?"

Her anger flared again.

"Look, Mr.—"

"Just call me Jack," he said. "I think I'd like that."

"Well, look, I—"

"You don't have to get so steamed up! Cripes, I only—"

"Dammit, will you stop interrupting me?" She breathed deeply and her dress filled out taut in front. "It's none of your business. I thought you just came here to get that transfer signed."

"Sure, that's right."

"Well, you got it signed." The corners of her mouth drooped disgustedly. "And you got your free look, didn't you? Now, why the hell don't you beat it?"

He hesitated just a moment and then he moved closer to her. Her throat got hot and dry and the walls of the room seemed to press together, bringing her nearer to him. She could almost feel what the heat of his body would be like, the strong, furious power of his arms around her. She wished that she had never left Harris, never sold the Buick, that this man hadn't bought the thing.

"Please," she said, uncertainly. "I wish you'd go."

"I know that."

"Then—why don't you?"

"I ought to."

Somebody moved a chair in the room next door and she could hear water running through the hot water pipes along the wall.

"I'll live to see the day I wished I had." His voice was slow and calm and a little afraid.

Her glance moved up his chest and across his face. The question was there in the shine of her eyes, the pout on her lips, the careless toss of her blonde hair.

"I think you're that kind of a woman," he said.

She hit him hard, with the flat of her right hand, across the side of his face. The white marks of her fingers blended with the scar, wiping it away.

"You are that kind of a woman," he said softly, a smile tugging at his lips. Then he walked over to the lounge chair and sat down. He leaned back, still smiling, only his eyes hard. "Baby, there's something you should know," he said. "I'm that kind of a guy."

She felt a little weak. Her fingers ached and they shook a trifle as she jammed the cigarette into an ash tray. But her confidence was coming back, flooding through her, because she knew that there had been a struggle there, for just a moment, and she knew that she had won. She didn't have to ask herself why it had turned out like that; she knew. This man was just the same as Mr. Rodney, or Roy. He was like the rest of them. He was after something that she had—something that he wasn't going to get.

"Did I tell you that I was in the roofing business?"

She nodded.

"Well, I'm a salesman. I don't mean I sell just roofs for houses and business buildings, but also sidewalls for homes. Mostly I sell shingle jobs to people who would normally paint the exterior of their houses. Saves money for them in the end—that kind of baloney, you know. Anyhow, this company I'm with is pretty big and a salesman has to be strictly on the ball to stay in their rat race. Do you follow me?"

"It sounds silly to me," Della said, leaning against the dresser. "I don't see why any company should need salesmen to sell those kind of things. If a person needs a new roof or—sidewall—they just look in the phone book and call somebody who's in the business."

"Yeah?"

"I'd think so."

"Della, how old are you?"

"Twenty."

"I thought so. People just don't act like that, Della."

"Maybe not. What difference does it make?"

"Now wait a minute; let me prove it to you," he said. "Can you ever remember when your father ever called on anyone about one of those things? To get your roof fixed? Or anything like that?"

She thought of the pots and pans that were scattered around the attic, the brown stains on the wall paper, the roof shingles that blew off with the slightest encouragement from a gentle breeze.

"I guess you answered my question," Jack Bishop said. He leaned farther back in his chair, put his hands behind his head and stared thoughtfully at her. "Now, Della, I know you're asking yourself what the hell is this guy talking about, aren't you?"

"Well," she admitted, "I'm having a little trouble keeping up with you."

"All right. Now, let me ask you something: do you want to work?"

"Don't be so stupid," she said. "Of course I don't want to work. But I have to."

"Baby," he said, "with your looks you wouldn't have to do a tap. You wouldn't have to do anything."

"Wouldn't I?" she challenged him.

"I think we could use you in the roofing and siding business," he said quickly. "You'd fit pretty good."

"I've never been on a ladder in my life," Della said. "And the only thing I've ever nailed down was my high school diploma."

"Whenever you decide to climb a ladder," he said, "just let me know and I'll hold it for you."

The way he was looking at her, and the way he said it, made her feel quite naked.

"I'll keep that in mind," she said.

"You're okay." He loosened his tie, sat up a little straighter. "You just listen to me, Della. You let your Uncle Jackson set you on the right road. That's no malarkey. I'm serious about you because I know you'd fit. I told you I was a salesman. I go to people's homes, demonstrate our product and stay until I get kicked out or make a sale. But before I can make any selling interviews I have to have prospects, people I can call on."

Della thought she was taking a long chance, but she was tired of standing. He occupied the only chair in the room, so she crossed over and sat on the bed.

"Now," he went on, watching the swing of her legs, "in order to get these people lined up we have to do a lot of cold canvassing. That means knocking on doors, talking to strange people. In our trade these people are called canvassers; the salesmen are known as closers. Very few closers do their own canvassing. Do you know why?"

She stopped swinging her legs. She wished she had put on a slip. The thin material of the dress slid across her thighs, down between her legs.

"Of course I don't know."

"Well, the answer is simple. If the closers did their own canvassing, they'd be so tired by the end of the day that they'd never go back to do the selling job. Besides, by doing both jobs themselves they lose much of their effectiveness. When making an appointment, the canvasser always refers to the closer as an expert—or the factory engineer—whether the guy has been selling the stuff two days or two years."

"And you think I might make—what?"

"A canvasser."

"I see."

"There's nothing to it."

"I've never done anything like that," she said. "What difference does that make?"

"I don't know. I'm just telling you, that's all."

"You'd do all right at it," he said, staring at her legs, at the curl of her toes. "Most of our business, in the final analysis, is done with men. It's easy for a woman—a beautiful woman—to make an appointment with men."

"That's all there is to it?" she asked. "Just making appointments?"

"Mostly, yes. But when I go back to sell, I always take the woman along. It helps. I usually spend most of my time talking directly to the woman of the house where I'm calling, and I let the girl talk to the man silently, showing him an inch of knee every now and then."

"You've had girls working for you before?"

"Sure, I've been in this racket for over ten years."

"It does sound like a racket."

"Well, what isn't?" he demanded, slightly perturbed. "Selling isn't what it used to be, you know. Not in any line. A few years back you went out and laid the facts on the line, tried to sell the things that your company would do, and had a legitimate conversation with your prospect. Today, you don't do that. You use psychology. You use tricks—anything inside or outside of the law—until you get your sucker in a corner and then you slam the contract on his head. The customers made it like this, so I guess that's the way they want it."

Della regarded him closely.

"I'm not thinking about the ethics," she told him. "That never entered my head."

"I knew that."

"Tell me about the other girls that worked with you."

He thought a minute.

"There was Agnes," he said. "She got married."

"And?"

"Stella," he said. He shook his head. "She took her job too seriously at impressing men and got pregnant."

Della yawned. "It sounds like a hazardous occupation," she said.

"Well, for gosh sake!" he said, getting up. He took a cigarette from his pocket and jammed it into his mouth. "I'm not asking you to sleep with anybody."

She watched him go over to the radio and turn the dial.

The music, soft and clear, filled the room. She had never met a man like him before, a man who could strip her thoughts to the framework and hold them up to ridicule. There had been Mr. Rodney, who had been dumb; Roy who had, in his own way, been afraid. There had been some others, too, but she couldn't remember now, and she didn't care who they had been. This man interested her, and she didn't particularly like that. But there wasn't very much that she could do about it.

He came back to the bed and stood directly over her. "There's nothing to it, Della. You just look like you do now and you make appointments for me."

"How about shoes?"

"You wear your shoes, or don't wear them. I don't give a damn."

"All right."

"I'll show you how it's done. After you get in the house you sit across from the man where he can see you. You may not be wearing a short dress, but you keep it high enough. In case you don't get past the door, your dress should be low-cut and full."

Her glance moved away from his face.

"With you," he said, "the full part won't be any problem at all."

The room started to close in on her again. He was bending over her now, closer this time, the nearness of him flooding through her.

"What's the next step, professor?" she murmured.

"That's all there is to it."

"It sounds easy enough."

"It is. And profitable."

"Well."

His lips brushed her hair and then he stood up straight. "What do you say?"

"I—don't know."

"But you'll think it over?"

"Yes."

"Think it over until tomorrow night," he said. "I'll come back tomorrow night and you can let me know."

She slid along the bed, rumpling the sheet, and stood up.

"That will be all right." She knew, even then, what her answer would be. "I'll let you know then."

She moved away from him quickly, the dress flowing around her hips, thrusting in at the empty feeling in her stomach. He started to follow her, then turned and went to the door. She did not look at him. Her breathing was rapid and strained. The points of her breasts, hard and aching, clawed at the thin material.

"Della," he said, "I'll be back tomorrow night."

She didn't say anything. She just leaned on the window sill, looking out and seeing nothing, feeling the dryness burn in her throat.

The door opened.

"Della," he said, softly. "Della, any time you want your shingles nailed on, just let me know."

The door closed behind him and he was gone.

Come back, she thought, as she turned, flushed and smiling, from the window. Come back. And bring your hammer.

4

The night and the lights came to the city again, only this time there was no fog and the air was sharp and clear. It had rained all day, starting with a thundershower early in the morning—too damn early!—and after that the sky had cleared, scarred only by white clouds driven by fresh winds.

That afternoon she had gone out and bought a new dress. Lord, how fast the money went! She had told herself that she needed the dress—she always looked good in something black—and that this Bishop guy didn't have anything to do with it. But she knew that he did. She had known it, there in the store while she'd been trying on the dress, making sure that it dipped far enough in front, came in snug around her hips.

"Thirty-eight!" the flat-chested woman had told her when she came out of the dressing-room. "My word!"

The flat-chested woman had had a nice face, a quiet face because it had lacked color, but the lines had been good and soft. That was the trouble with most women, Della thought. They didn't spend enough time improving what they had, put too much effort into trying to copy what another woman had. A woman saw another woman with a good shape, and then she'd go out and buy a pair of false bumpers and try to kid every man that came along. But they couldn't kid the men, because the men wouldn't keep their hands where they belonged, and so these women drew attention to what they didn't have, which made it better for girls like Della.

She looked into her pocketbook but she didn't bother counting the money. She knew what was there. Twenty-five dollars and a dollar credit slip she could use the next time she had her hair done. That was a laugh! With hair like this, she thought, glancing in the mirror, she should pay some Willie for messing it up. That was like a guy buying hair restorer from a bald-headed barber.

She thought about the money again. She had intended to send her father the amount of his original investment in the car. But she'd put it off, waited too long. Well, she could send it the next week. Or the week after. Or in a couple of years.

She walked to the window and the darkness was out there, hiding the city. Down on the corner a guy and a girl stood arguing and the girl had her hand on one of the guy's arms. He started to walk away, but the girl said something to him and he stopped, then put his arm around her waist and they went down the street and out of sight. Another man, much older, came along and stood watching after them. Pretty soon he went into the all-night restaurant on the corner, and as he opened the door music from a juke-box came out and filled the shadows.

What time was Jack Bishop coming? Maybe he wouldn't come. Well, to hell with him! No, that wasn't right. She could say that and she could think it, but it wasn't the way she felt. She knew how she felt. She'd been feeling like that all day. Waiting for him. Hoping that he would come. Primarily, she knew, there was nothing physical about it. Of course, she liked him. He'd interested her. But there was more to it than that. There was the job that sounded easy and paid good for what you had to put into it. And jobs, real jobs, were scarce; she'd found that out.

That morning there'd been an ad in the paper, a good sounding ad, and she'd gone down there early to this wholesale grocery place, skipping her coffee. The place had been near the railroad yards, in a red brick building that looked dirty even after the savage shower.

One man had been in the place, a fairly young man with a thin, white face and a skinny frame. Yes, he was the owner and he'd had the ad put in the paper for a typist. He just had a small business, not much to do. Then he'd come out from behind the cage and he'd seen Della standing with her back to the open door and he'd coughed a couple of times. Naturally, he'd pointed out, there was some night work—he was on the road two or three days a week and he had to work nights to catch up. Did she understand him? Yes, she understood him—perfectly. For that he paid twenty-seven a week and periodic bonuses.

The son-of-a-buck, she thought now. A man like that should take a trip to Harris every week or so, or just ask a taxi driver.

She wondered what time Jack Bishop would come.

Would he like the dress? Certainly he'd like the dress. And these half-slips were all right. She'd never had one before. The only things they'd had at the store in Harris were bloomers and long-johns. And the brassiere! That wasn't comfortable at all. She wished that she'd left it off.

There wasn't much light in the room, just a little from the forty-watt floor lamp in the corner. She started to pull the dress up over her head, then remembered what the woman in the store had told her.

"You'd better buy one, dearie. That material is sheer—real sheer—and if you don't, you'll look like a dog with pups."

She left it on.

Dammit, she thought, he's not coming. It must be after eight. Maybe he's working. Or maybe he found something else. She laughed quietly. Men were such fools. They talked about love—and what did they mean? They meant only what the animals meant, but they put it in different words, wrapped it up in presents, bought it with money, just trying to make it look like something different, dreaming up any vague excuse for getting what they wanted.

Sex, she thought. Male and female. A virgin or a whore. A pimp or a banker. A movie actress or a duchess. A boy and a girl. Was there so much difference in what they did? Was there?

And would they—the virgin, or the banker, or the duchess, or the boy and girl—admit that it was just a medium of exchange? Naturally they wouldn't. They were civilized, they talked, they dressed up in clothes—when they weren't doing the thing they didn't want to talk about—and they went to finishing schools, to the board meetings, to the king's court, to schools or to colleges. They played golf on Sundays, went to church, sang in the choir, drank whiskey, beat hell out of their kids, made the insurance man come back a couple of times to get his money—and they were civilized by virtue of the fact that they could do all these human things. And all the time they would say that they weren't trading. What a joke! What a plain lie!

Of course they were trading—doing most of it in bed, and not admitting it. The whore who traded a few minutes of her time to earn money with the banker who was lonely and who swapped his money for the touch of a woman. The movie actress who looked at the director, at the director's bed, and made a split decision, both of them trading because they wanted to get a little something of what the other had. The boy and the girl who, deep in the shadows of the back seat of a car, traded with each other because it was new, and they were afraid, and they wanted knowledge and had to do some exchanging to get it. And the man and wife, the people who loved each other, who bought a house or a new car and worked together to pay for it—they traded in bed, too. They bartered affection, the nearness of each other—and if they couldn't find it they got a divorce and they said they were incompatible. They would hire lawyers and the lawyers would know what they meant. The whole bunch of them would get up in front of a judge, using nice words, and the judge would know what they meant, too. Everybody knew. Everybody who read the account in the paper, or who walked down the street or who took a breath the next day, knew exactly what was meant. And no one would say. Because they were a lovely couple and wasn't it a terrible shame they couldn't get along? But they wouldn't use the right words, they wouldn't put the facts on the line where everybody knew they belonged. After all, people wore clothes, didn't they?

Steps came along the hall, passed her door and went into the room beyond. Why didn't he come? Twenty-five dollars wouldn't last long. She shouldn't have bought the dress, and the money she'd tossed away on her hair—she'd have to stop doing things like that.

Knocking on doors didn't sound very difficult. She thought that Jack Bishop might be interesting to work with. And she had read that selling was about the highest paid work.

She started to laugh, a little shocked at the reasons she was thinking up.

She was no different from the other people who wore clothes.

She wouldn't put a name on it.

All right, she thought, why don't I admit it? I think that sex—as an act—is greatly overrated, if not a colossal flop. Sometimes it had more value than a dozen bank accounts and sometimes it wasn't worth as much as last night's effort. It was simply a matter of judgment, of just being sure that nothing was ever given away simply for the experience of giving it.

The knock was loud and sharp at her door. She let him wait a couple of seconds and then she went over and opened it.

"Hi, Della!"

He came in, his grin flashing. He was dressed in blue slacks and a gray sport coat. His blue shirt was open at the throat.

"I thought you weren't coming," she said.

His glance was sharp.

"I had a hell of a day!"

The door sucked closed.

"That's too bad."

"Thanks."

"I'm just saying it."

"Baby!" he said, jamming his hands into his pockets. "Baby, I think I've had it! I made three selling interviews and got nothing."

She didn't know what he was talking about.

"That last one!" he groaned. "That was on Erie Street. You know, near the oil tanks."

"No."

"Well, it's not far from here—in distance. In looks—it's out of this world. It's near the railroad and gets plenty of smoke, making the outside of the houses black and crummy."

"That ought to be good for the siding business."

"I've sold a lot of jobs down there," he said. "But this one was tough. They were Italian and I went back there about four-thirty this afternoon. I'd been around there in the morning, cold canvassing by myself. Doing that always burns me up, and I missed asking the guy's wife a couple of leading questions."

"You said that was hard," she, reminded him. "Doing both."

He nodded and sat down on the edge of the bed. Della went over and leaned against the dresser.

"She was a good-looking wench—the wife," he said reflectively. "She kept smiling at me all the time—that was this morning. When I went back this afternoon, she still smiled—but at her husband, or at least so the poor slob would think she was smiling at him. This guy grunts and tells me how hot it is working on the railroad tracks, and I agree once in a while and give him my demonstration. Then, just as I got ready to close the sale I found out that they didn't own the house. Yipes!"

"You did have a tough day," she said.

He shrugged and dug out cigarettes.

"It happens. That's the trouble with selling. You can have a nightmare right in the daytime." He looked through the smoke at her. "Lord, but you're beautiful," he said.

He was like all the rest, she thought. He was looking for something. And he couldn't think of a new way to go about it.

"You've thought about what I asked you last night?"

"Some."

"And?"

"I don't know," Della said. She knew—she had known last night—but he was going to work for it.

"We'd make a good team," he said earnestly, moving around on the bed. "You'd knock 'em dead."

"It isn't that."

"What then?"

"Well—"

"It isn't like selling magazines," he said. "You read about that in the papers, how the girls knock on doors of hotel rooms and that kind of stuff. This is different. This is dealing with home owners—not that they don't get the same ideas, but their wives are there and they can't do much about it."

"It's the money," Della said. "That's what I've been thinking about. You didn't say how much."

"Oh, that."

"It comes in handy."

"Fifty a week," he told her. "Fifty a week advance against commissions, and you get as much out of each sale as I do. We split the take right down the middle. All you have to do is talk nice to the people and act pretty. Neither one should be very hard."

"It doesn't sound so bad," she admitted.

"About the advance—you don't have to worry over that. A lot of people think that an advance is a loan. In a way it is. But if you worked for Wyandot a couple of months and you never made a sale, they couldn't get a nickel back. You could tell them that you were out there, every day, talking Wyandot and that they got a lot of advertising—so what more would they want? All you have to do is be sure that you keep talking up the company."

"What else would I talk about?"

He grinned.

"You'd be surprised, Della. We've had guys and girls on drawing accounts who wandered around never talking roofs or sidewalls, but selling insurance or silverware. I remember one guy who was peddling a new clothesline that didn't need any pins on it. He crossed himself up and tried to sell one to Hank Annabella's wife. Hank happened to be home at the time."

"Who's Annabella?"

"I didn't tell you?" He got up, went to the table and stubbed out his cigarette in the ash tray. "No, I guess I didn't. He's the boss."

"Oh," she said, disappointed. "I thought you did the hiring."

"We hire our own canvassers—if we have confidence in them." His long stare tried to remove her dress. "And I've got confidence in you. Plenty!"

"That's nice."

"Well, what do you say?"

"I could try it," she said.

"I knew you would," he said, and came over close to her.

Her chin lifted.

"How did you know?"

"I just did," he said. "It had to be like that."

He moved closer to her, and her back hurt where the sharp edge of the dresser dug into her flesh. She felt his hands reaching down and coming around her middle, swift and gentle. She turned a little, moving away from him, and his hands fell free.

"I'm still thinking about it," she said huskily.

"Okay, okay."

The guy next door was drawing water again, the pipe thumping with the steam. Somebody was out in the hall, shouting; a door slammed and it was quiet again.

"I'll give you an idea how you go about it," he said. "It's simple enough."

"Well—all right."

He went quickly to the door, his broad shoulders swaying. For the first time she noticed how slim his hips were.

"I'll just go out in the hall, knock, and you open the door. We can go on from there."

She nodded as the door opened and closed behind him.

For just a few moments she was alone in the room. Thoughts flashed through her mind like tape through a high-speed cash register. Fifty dollars a week and half of the commission on each, sale which was the result of any lead she gave him. What the hell could go wrong on a deal like that? That was better than walloping a typewriter for an old guy like Layton or slamming dishes around some broken-down restaurant. Maybe, even, she would be able to get more out of Jack than just the fifty-fifty profit from each sale. Considering what he might spend on her, she might be able to work it up to seventy-five percent.

His knock rattled the door. She went to it, her hips rolling, pulling her dress down hard across the cleft between her breasts. She put a smile on her lips, the stars in her eyes, and pulled the door open.

"Oh, good evening!" he said, cheerfully. His grin flashed and his eyes didn't miss a thing. "Miss Banners, my name is Jack Bishop, and I'm associated with the Wyandot Roofing Company. Perhaps you have noticed the beautiful exterior of the Ross property on Elm Street?"

"Oh, of course," she said, picking up her cue. "Who hasn't?"

"Well, that's one of our jobs." She hadn't been aware of it, but he had moved forward steadily and now he was inside the room. "Your house could look like that, too, you know."

"I don't think I'd be, interested in anything like that," she said.

"You mean, you don't want a house that looks as nice as that?"

"Well, sure, only—"

"Look, Miss Banners, I really didn't think that you'd be

in the market right now. That's the truth. But some day you'll want to paint the outside of this place, won't you? That is, if you do own the house. You do own the house, don't you?"

Della smiled at him prettily.

"Oh, yes, I own the house," she said. "But spending money on it right now is out of the question."

"I haven't asked you to spend any money, have I, Miss Banners?"

"No—but you're a salesman."

"A factory representative," he corrected her, spreading his hands wide. "There's a difference."

"Well, I don't know about those things."

"A lot of people don't," he agreed. "But even though I were a salesman, that wouldn't induce you to spend, or to stop you from spending, money on this house some day, would it?"

"I suppose not."

"The paint's chipped on the outside."

"You don't have to tell me."

"And it's all peeled under the eaves,"

"I know that, too."

"Painting would cost a lot of money," he said. "You'd be surprised how much it would cost today."

"What doesn't?"

"I guess you're right," he admitted.

He was now standing in the middle of the room. She wished that she could remember how he'd done it. She had heard, and read, that the first rule of the house sales-man was to get inside; Jack Bishop didn't miss a trick when it came to that.

"There's no use taking up your time," she said.

"But you're not taking up my time, Miss Banners," he protested. "The company pays me by the house. That is, I am not a salesman—as I told you. They give me so many houses to cover in a day, and that's the basis on which I get paid. I'm just a visitor, as the company calls me—or, if you prefer, a factory representative. We don't have any salesmen. When we talk with someone, like yourself, who needs to have work done, we arrange—if it's satisfactory to you—to have one of our siding and roofing experts call on you and explain our services—our services which are guaranteed for twenty years. Do I make myself clear?"

"I think you do," Della said. "But I don't think that I did. I simply can't consider spending any money right now."

"But you will have to have something done some day?" His voice held an earnest appeal. "Won't you, Miss Banners?"

"Naturally," she said, then instantly realized that she had stepped into his trap.

"I don't know why I couldn't get that thought of yours into words, but that's exactly what I meant," he said, bringing the jaws of the trap shut. "Since our expert is also paid by the number of people he talks to—whether they do anything about their problems right now or not—I am going to be very blunt and suggest that I bring him around to speak with you. He can give you expert advice, thinking in terms of your needs and your means available to meet those needs. What would be the best time for you? This evening, say around seven, or tomorrow evening about the same time?"

"Well, I'm going out tonight, and—"

"Fine! We'll see you tomorrow night at seven."

Neat, she thought, very neat. No real pressure, yet it was there all the time, digging away at the prospect.

"That's all there is to it," Jack told her. "Nothing more than that. Doesn't that sound like an easy job?"

"Yes."

"But it has to be done right."

"I can see that."

He frowned and handed her a cigarette.

"I missed one thing, though. You have to watch out for it. Of course, I addressed you as Miss Banners—but it still wasn't right. Maybe you lived with your mother, or an old aunt, or just some guy—and these people help you make your decisions. You have to be extremely careful about that. If it's a married couple, be sure that both of them are going to be there when you go back. You have to have everybody present, during the interview, who is going to have a voice in making the decision. If you don't, the one you're talking to will want to think it over—and thinking is always bad."

"What happens if you can't get in when you go back?" she asked, breathing deep of the smoke.

"Don't let that worry you," he said, "There'll be times like that. But the average will hold up. It's mostly a question of selling yourself and building up your factory expert. Keep bearing down on that expert business. People love that—they like to feel important. That's one way of doing it."

"Well," she said, blowing the smoke out and smiling at him, "it sounds pretty much okay. When do I start?"

"How about tomorrow?"

"What time?"

"Around nine. The boss gets in around that time, and we can go down and meet him. He'll put you on the payroll and we can start right out."

"You'll have to show me," she said.

He went over and closed the door, then came back to her again. The hot water thumped in the pipes again and down in the street a couple of cars fought a duel with their horns.

"I'll show you," he said.

She stubbed out the cigarette, not looking at it, and the tip of one finger burned sharply.

"We aren't on company time now," he said as his cigarette joined hers in the ash tray. "We're on our own."

The room started to grow smaller again, and the needles were at her spine, shooting out all through her body. He put his hands on her waist, and she didn't move this time. She was like a tiny piece of steel being gathered up by a large magnet. She was conscious of the tightness of her dress, the sticky dampness under her arms, the dim table light which seemed to burn bright and hot.

"We've got plenty of time," he said, his hands finding her. "Nothing but—"

"Please!" she whispered, suddenly afraid. "You're hurting me."

One hand loosened and slid around to the small of her back, passed down and over her buttocks. She started to tremble. She wanted to cry. She was scared to death. And she hadn't been afraid with Mr. Rodney, or Roy. But with this man she was frightened. And she knew why.

He was the first man she had ever wanted.

His hand was stretched out far behind him now, fumbling for the lamp. She heard the chain rattle. Then his body was pushed up against her hard as he made a final grab, and the light clicked off.

The room became a dark, hollow shell, lighted only by the weak rays of the street light below that peeked up through the rain-specked window.

"How lovely you are!" he whispered hoarsely.

She thought of a movie projection room in a high school auditorium and of a man who stood and cried. She supposed that she would never forget that, because they said you never forgot the first one. And she thought of Roy, too, because she had loved Roy and he had torn her dress and she had been sore about that.

Jack's face came toward her, out of the shadows, and his mouth found her lips, wiping away the thoughts, bringing the ache all through her. The skin on his face was soft under her hands and she could tell, just by feeling, that his eyes were closed.

"I'll help you with your dress," he said softly. "Please let me help you."

He was gentle, making sure that the zipper did not bite into her flesh. He hung the dress over the lamp and then his hands were at her back, fumbling, hurting her for just a moment, as he loosened the brassiere. It fell away from her, and came down over her arms, leaving her breasts naked and hard and thrusting out at him.

"Lord!" he breathed.

He turned her a little and then she was in his arms, just the two of them in the room and the night all around them. The bed was near and pretty soon they went over there and he kissed her again. She sat down on the bed, in her slip, wondering if she ought to take off her stockings but not caring too much about them. He was in the shadows and she saw him take off his coat.

Quietly he came to her on the bed, his breathing heavy, his hands seeking and finding and knowing her. The heat of the room became the cooling breeze that touched them as they shared this moment together—this moment that belonged to them alone.

Later, she lay there panting, unable to move and thinking of only one thing. This, she thought, could be love. This was being possessed by a man, possessing him. They were two people becoming one. This was what she had been waiting for since that afternoon at school, since that night along the Willowkill. This was being wanted.

The mattress of the bed rose sharply as he swung his long legs over the side and got to his feet. Della continued to lie there, wanting him to hold her tight again, to tell her that she was the same now as she had been a few minutes before.

"I'm sorry, Della," he said, softly. "I'm really sorry."

She turned her head and looked up at his blurred shape. "Are you?"

"Well—sure."

This bed could have been that old box of films, the night could have been the fog along the stream. There was no difference. They were the same.

"I wish you wouldn't cry," he said.

She laughed, bitterly, and the salt of her tears touched and stung her lips.

"Don't spoil it," she said in a small voice. "Don't say anything."

He stood perfectly still.

"I've got to go," he said.

"I didn't say so—Jack."

"No."

"But you will."

He went to the door, opened it and closed it again. He started to walk back to the bed, then stopped.

"I should have told you, Della," he said. A match flared and the tip of his cigarette burned brightly. "I'm married, baby."

The silence came into the room, tearing them apart.

"I've got to pick my wife up from the movies," he said. He opened the door again. "I'll be back in the morning, Della."

"I don't give a simple damn if you never come back!" she said into the pillow.

The door closed and he was gone. She heard his footsteps go down the hall. She started to cry, real hard—not because of what had happened, but because of what she had said.

She wanted him to come back and stay there with her in that bed forever.

5

The Wyandot Roofing Company was located an obscure building on a side street of doubtful character. On the front of the building snow-white shingles constantly reminded the passing public how a beautiful home might look. A huge sign advertised the name of the firm in proud black letters. The casual passerby, quite naturally, would assume that Wyandot shingles remained always as white as those on display. No one, of course, publicized the fact that a new front was applied to the structure almost every six months.

Della had been working for Wyandot two weeks before she drew her initial paycheck. She had raised hell with the cashier that first Friday when there hadn't been any money for her. The fact that the company made a rule of holding back the first week's pay hadn't soothed her—the hotel hadn't been inclined to believe her yarn that she was working—but she didn't give a damn about that now, because Jack had paid her hotel bill and she had a nice fat check in her hands.

"Not bad," she told Miss Johnson. "Not bad at all."

The check was for one hundred sixty-nine dollars and seventeen cents. Actually, her pay had been considerably more, but there were deductions. She wondered if she could claim her father and mother as dependents and if she would have to send them money if she did that. There was also a small amount taken out for her old age which, heaven knew, she'd never live to see, anyway.

Miss Johnson stared through her glasses at Della. She was an old maid with long gray-black hair tied in a severe knot at the back of her neck. She had a small, withered body that never seemed to fit in the center of the dresses which she wore. She was, by habit, suspicious of all young girls—and all men, whether young or old. She had replaced her niece, a couple of years back, when the younger girl had refused to sleep with Mr. Annabella, the office manager. Mr. Annabella had never given Miss Johnson a chance to refuse a request like that.

"That's more than any canvasser ever made here before," Miss Johnson said. "And there's been a lot of them. But that's the most."

Della looked back into the stern face, saw that her body was being appraised, inch by inch, just as though she had climbed into bed with every prospect she'd met.

"But I guess you earned it," Miss Johnson said.

"On my feet," Della told her.

"It's too bad that you weren't dressed," Miss Johnson pointed out acidly, and turned her back.

Della shrugged, stuck out her tongue, and put away the check. Well, to hell with her! The old bitch!

The outer office of Wyandot was small, neat and gleaming. There were two windows at the short counter. One was marked Paying and the other Receiving. Here the canvassers and the closers drew their pay every Friday morning. And here the customers of Wyandot came to pay their bills, register their complaints and get sassed by Miss Johnson.

Della went through a small door and entered the salesroom. This was a bare hole in the wall with some chairs, an old ping pong table with soda bottles and ash trays piled on top, a blackboard and a couple of dirty windows. On the blackboard a progress chart of the sales of canvassers and closers was listed, starting with high man on top. Della noticed that her name was the fourth one down. A few men were gathered around the chart and some women lounged nearby, smoking or fixing their faces.

"Hey, there, Della!"

Len Parks, a big square-set man in his late thirties, broke

away from the group of men and came over to her. His reddish face had a stubble of beard on it and his gray suit needed pressing. Also, he had been wearing the same green coffee-spotted tie since the first day Della had met him.

"Hi, Len!"

"Seen Jack this morning?"

She shook her head and the smile left her face.

"Still on it," Len said. "Won't he ever learn?"

Len didn't look very much like a salesman, but Della had turned a couple of leads over to him—after Jack had gone on his bender and she'd had no closer to work with—and Len had closed both of them. However, just this morning she had found a note in her mail box curtly informing her that one of the jobs wanted to cancel out.

"That Simpson wants to cancel," Della said.

Len grinned, displaying a couple of chipped front teeth.

"That was before eight-thirty this morning, Della. I came in early, found my note and went right down to see him. I told him, pointblank, that we couldn't do the job."

"Oh, no!" Della gasped. That had been a thousand dollar job. What if Simpson's house was so old that he couldn't get a couple of thousand for it, lock, stock and cellar? That was no skin off her knees. Fifteen percent of a thousand dollar contract meant a hundred and fifty bucks, and half of that meant a nice piece of change for Della.

"He comes to the door and I throw it right in his face," Len said. "I tell him that we can't do any business with him because he's such a lousy credit risk. I tell him that the company wouldn't sell him a two-by-four on time. I give him hell because he hadn't been honest with us and that he'd put us to so much work for nothing."

"Was that the reason?"

"Hell, no!" Len said. "But it made him sore. He said, by cripes he'd always paid his bills and I'd better come in and talk to his wife. I told him to forget about it, but he grabs me by the arm and I go inside the shack. He tells his wife about it and they both jump on me. They say they have good credit. I argue with them. And you know what happens?"

"They want the job done," Della said. "They want that job more than they ever wanted anything else in their lives before."

"Sure, that's it. Then I tell them that if I can get a couple of siding men down, without the boss knowing, and nail on four or five shingles, why the contract'll be in force and the company'll have to go along on the job. So I get Hype James and Willie Adams—I had them up here waiting for my call—to come down, quick-like, and slap some shingles on that goat's nest."

Della's eyes lit in admiration. She reached up and gave Len a pat on one cheek.

"Just like that!"

"Yeah."

"You're smooth, Len."

"In this business you've got to be," he told her. "Maybe you're doing the right thing for people, and maybe you're doing the wrong thing. You musn't ever worry about that. Just look upon them as suckers. Don't worry about them. If they're old enough to vote, they're old enough to take care of themselves. You just take care of Della Banners and that's all you have to worry about."

Her glance met his steadily.

"I'll take care of myself," she said.

"I had an idea you would," Len said.

Della glanced around. She knew most of these people. There was Ed Barnes, slim, shallow looking, who was in his middle twenties and already had four children, none whom he refused to claim. Then there was Ben Kasselman who wouldn't sell a Wyandot job to a Jew because he didn't want to stick his own people, and who had trouble selling to other people because they thought he was trying to take them. And there was Charlie Short, who came to work drunk and went home in the same condition. There was a big fellow named Ray Michaels and a newcomer whose name Della couldn't remember. A couple of guys had quit since she'd started, but their names were still up there on the blackboard, listed somewhere in the group of names headed by Jack Bishop.

And, of course, there were the girls. There was Billie Norton, blonde, hard-faced, with a good shape from Best Form and a disposition as brittle as a dry stick. Annie Bolton was slim, dark-haired; she lived with a plumber who was not her husband and who plumbed at his work only during those periods when Annie had a bad run of sales. She seemed to be quite friendly with Jo Ann Hale, a fair-skinned brunette, who wore different sized falsies in the daytime than she did at night—bigger by day. Janice Denton was smaller than the others, homelier because of her large front teeth and small, angry appearing face, but popular with the salesmen and countless prospects due to certain perverted favors which she bestowed without preference.

"Remember," Len told her, moving away, "you're in this business to make money. That's all."

More than that, she thought, much more than that. Of course there was money in this racket, plenty of money—and, she supposed, getting right down to it, that's all there was. But, whatever else there might be, whatever went with it, she wanted it, too—after, of course, the money.

She thought about the manager, Hank Annabella. He must be doing all right—even after you got a Caddy it took dough to run one. Hank always had his eyes on her legs and his mind above the hem of her dress. And the big shot from New York—that vice president named Cord, the middle-aged guy who wore the tweeds—had mentally kept getting into bed with her that day he was up for the sales conference.

They're like the rest, she thought—like Roy and Mr. Rodney and Jack, too. Except that they have more money and if they get something they can pay for it. That's a difference in men, she thought—some pay and some don't. Not in money, exactly. Because a girl didn't take money unless she was a tramp, or a mistress, or a fool. But a girl could take the things that men could do for her, use these things to her advantage—making money, or social standing, or anything else—and that was all right. That was, Della felt, just being smart.

No more Rodneys, no more Roys, no more Jacks— well, not many Jacks, anyway—just the kind of guys from whom there would be something left the next morning, something that had been worth the effort. From now on that was the way it was going to be.

Ben Kasselman joined her.

"Sorry about Jack, Della."

"How are you, Ben?" She shrugged her shoulders, said before he could answer, "I haven't seen Jack in a week."

That first week Jack had been good, so helpful, and he had worked like a machine, closing sales that had seemed almost impossible. Then the night he had paid her hotel bill he had come up to her room with her, but she had made him stay out in the hall, finally closing the door on him. He hadn't been to work since.

"I'm telling you," Ben said, "he's a crazy guy. But don't worry about him. He's only got to be sober a month out of the year to do as much as the rest of us. I know he got you to come down here and you must be sorry about him, but you shouldn't worry."

"I'm not, Ben."

"Nah, nah," he said, patting her shoulder. "Don't lie to me. Just forget it."

"All right, Ben."

She wished that she could forget Jack. She wanted to

forget that night, and how gentle he had been and that he was married. She wished desperately he'd sober up and come back to work. Len was all right, but Jack was a better closer and she wanted the best because she wanted the most out of this business.

"He'll be back," Ben said, "as soon as he's broke."

Della fluffed her hair with one hand. The soft, rounded front of her dress shook and Ben wagged his head.

"If I was him, I wouldn't have stayed so long now," he said.

Della gave Ben a smile and turned and went over to where the girls were sitting.

"Hello, working girls," Della said. "How's your shingles today?"

"I wondered what blew off my head last night," Billie stated, massaging her scalp. "Cripes, what a hoe-down!"

"Tough customer?" Della wanted to know.

"That had all the elements of a dirty crack."

"Oh, come off it," Jo Ann begged them. She glanced around and yawned. "When in hell are they going to start this meeting? I could go to sleep right now. Why do they have to hold meetings in the morning, anyway? Why don't they do it at night when everybody is awake?"

"Don't be bitter," Della said. She regarded the circles under Jo Ann's eyes, the petulant droop of her mouth. "Ever try sleeping?"

"Not alone," Billie answered for her.

Jo Ann leaned back in the folding wooden chair, yawned again and stretched expansively. The falsies stood out pretty good.

"Gee, he was nice," she said, dreamily. "I've never been out with him before. And do you want to know something, you over-stacked females? I wasn't even wearing them last night. And he didn't care!"

"You see?" Billie demanded of no one in particular. "It pays to be honest."

Jo Ann was looking in admiration at the new closer who was staring at the tip of his shoes. Della wondered what the new man thought of Jo Ann this morning. She thought, too, that he was pretty good looking, in a serious type of way. He had narrow shoulders and a slim body. His face was thin and his hair sandy and rather long. Then Della noticed his hands and she lost all further interest in him. He was wearing nail polish.

A dirty-faced mechanic stuck his head in through the side door and yelled:

"Della Banners! Is Della Banners here?"

"Is she here?" Charlie Short wanted to know, staring at Della's tight fitting black-and-white check dress. "Are you kidding?"

Only the men laughed. The girls just sat there, as if nothing had been said. Della felt her face burn a little as she went over to the door. But she knew that her hips were swaying back and forth just right, and that made her feel good.

"I'm Della," she said.

"Fellow wants to see you," the man said. "Outside."

Della followed him out into the cinder-covered alley that separated the Wyandot Roofing Company and the Logan Burial Vault Company. She blinked her eyes against the glare of the bright sun and looked around. All she could see were concrete vaults stored on one side of the alley and huge piles of different-colored shingles on the other side.

"Della!"

He was sitting on a roll of tar paper, his chin in his hands, knees pulled up under him. Slowly, he got to his feet. His face was covered with a dark growth of heavy beard and she noticed that his hands were dirty. He wore an old pair of gray-colored slacks and a brown sport shirt. There was a big cut on one side of his jaw.

"You look like hell," she told him.

"I'm not drunk," he said, belligerently.

"I didn't say you were."

"But you were thinking it."

She stood very still, hardly breathing, as he walked up to her.

"Well, weren't you?"

"You wouldn't be here, if you knew what I was thinking," she said.

The anger slid out of his eyes, leaving only the dull hurt. "I'm sorry to bother you, Della."

"I'll bet you are."

His big bulk pushed up against her, and she retreated into the tiny corner that was created by the junction of the main building and the storage shed.

"I told Jimmy not to say who it was looking for you."

They stood there like that for a moment, very close together in the cool, mid-morning shadows, quiet and not saying a word. Their eyes fought a sharp duel, but it was Della who looked down first.

"You're a mess, Jack," she murmured. "You ought to be ashamed of yourself. If you could only see what you look like!"

"The damn car broke down. Honest, Della. It stopped right in the middle of the street. I had to push it out of the way by hand, and then I had to fix the carburetor. It runs all right now, though."

"Don't blame the car," she said. "That didn't take you a week. You've been hitting the booze."

"So?"

"That's not very smart, Jack. You ought to know that. You've tried it enough."

"What did you expect?" he demanded, pushing her deeper into the corner. "What did you think that I might do after you closed the door in my face?"

"That's something!" Della said, her eyes flashing up at him. "That's one all right. What do you think I am? Just a quick—"

"Baby, don't say that!"

"Well, you know what I mean," she said. "You know damned well."

"But it isn't that," he protested. "It isn't that at all. I like you, Della. Honest. And after that first time I felt so miserable, so rotten. It was one of those things that shouldn't have happened."

"You're still drunk," she said. "Or you wouldn't be talking like this."

He shook his head.

"And married," she said.

"That's the part—"

"That you forgot."

"No. I'm remembering that. Because of you, Della." He looked down at his dirty hands. "I couldn't help myself."

The smell of gasoline and grease came off his clothes and hung around them.

"Just start hoping one thing," she told him. "Just hope that I don't turn up pregnant."

"Holy Peter!"

"Does that sound so impossible?"

He sucked in his breath.

"That's all that has to happen," he said.

Until that moment she had been laughing at him, secure in her threats. But now, suddenly, she shared his fear and it seemed to form an instant bond between them, a sort of an unholy alliance. She looked at Jack and shuddered. What a hell of a thing to think about! Why, he didn't have a dime to his name.

"There's a sales meeting inside," Della said, weakly. "I'd better go, Jack."

"Sure."

"Well—so long."

He stood aside.

"I'll see you, baby."

She walked past him, not seeing him, not wanting to look at her. She was almost to the door when he caught up with her.

"Cripes, Della, I forgot what I wanted to see you about."

She stopped, not turning, afraid to have him see her face just then.

"I'll be back to work in a couple of days—just as soon as I get myself straightened out. But right now I need a little money. Could you help me out? I'll pay you back next week. Hank's got a week of my dough now, but he won't give it to me."

"How much do you want?"

"Fifty."

"I couldn't, Jack."

"Well, twenty-five."

"Not to drink with."

"Nope. Just expenses for next week."

"All right," Della said, jerking the door open. "You come to work Monday morning and I'll have it for you."

He was still swearing when she went in and closed the door.

6

Hank Annabella was practically doing handstands in the middle of the salesroom floor. He was down on both knees, his huge stomach having mysteriously disappeared somewhere, panting like a bellows on a forge while he talked. He had a hammer in one hand and there was a shingle lying flat on the floor in front of him.

"When you hit the damned shingle," he said, his big face red and perspiring, "be sure that it's flat on the floor. Like this, see? Remember, you're trying to impress your client that Wyandot shingles will not break, even when struck a terrific blow. But you have to have the shingle flat. You have the shingle any other way and you're going to embarrass yourself—and the company."

Charlie Short snickered.

"Hell, I didn't know that was possible," Charlie said.

"Well, Charlie, if you break the shingle—"

"So, all right," Charlie growled. "I bust the shingle. Then I give my people a big grin and tell them that that's one Wyandot replaces free."

"Why go to all that trouble?"

"I don't know," Charlie admitted. "But I do it once in a while."

Everybody laughed. Hank Annabella frowned and held up his hand.

"Can it, will you? I'd think that you people would want to listen to something that might help you. Look at that progress chart! Have you looked at it? We'll be lucky if we finish this quarter in the same class with Nome, Alaska."

"Hank's worried," Ben Kasselman said. "About his bonus. How about that, boss?"

"When you guys and dolls make money, I make money," Hank admitted, "And when you folks starve—I still eat. Remember that."

"Okay."

Hank used the hammer handle as a lever and pushed himself upright. His stomach appeared again, filling his green pants. He made a big fuss about brushing some dirt off his clothes and then he waddled up to the front of the room.

"The next five minutes will be devoted to gripes," he said, rubbing a white handkerchief across his forehead, down his face and around his neck. "Let's have them."

"You know, Hank," Ray Michaels said, "you ought to stop chewing the closers all the time. We don't always slice the cheese the wrong way. Some of these canvassers you get for us don't know a prospect from a corpse. Take that old man Wister you fired the other day. He'd get a lead and give it to every closer in the office. Then the closers just knocked themselves out, chasing each other around."

"That guy is history," Hank said, impatiently. "Forget it."

"I'm just telling you, that's all, Hank."

"I've been told."

"About the canvassers, I mean," Ray insisted.

In the short time which Della had been with Wyandot, she had learned the fact that the closer always held the canvasser to blame. The closer might be drunk, or insulting, or lose a sale because he tried to kiss the wrong woman, but all failures became the sole responsibility of the canvasser.

"A lot of times it is the canvasser," Len said. "You know that, Hank."

"I'll go along with that to a certain extent," Hank stated, half sitting on one corner of the ping pong table. "But, right now, I think we've got some pretty good canvassers. Billie over there could talk her way through a brick wall. Annie is the slow, confidential type who gets along with complaining housewives very well. And Jo Ann is especially good in the medium class neighborhoods where you can't be too fast or too slow with people. I don't know just what qualifications Janice has, and I don't care, because not many characters get away from her. Naturally, I know there is some danger in canvassing only with girls—some women resent the presence of a good looking wench in the house. But I'm going to change that when I latch onto a couple of good men one of these days."

Della felt a catch in her throat. She knew that she had been doing an outstanding job. And he hadn't even mentioned her name.

"I've got an idea that you left somebody out," Len Parks

said. "Personally, I think that Della Banners is the best canvasser that we've got."

There was a moment of silence.

"And I think that you're wrong," Hank said slowly.

Hank Annabella's eyes made a circle of the room, came back and rested on Della. She brought her knees together and pushed her skirt down. His gaze lifted past her face and regarded the ceiling.

"Della isn't a canvasser any more," Hank said. "I'm making Della a closer."

Della felt a surge of triumph.

"Oh!" she said.

Hank grinned at her.

"We've never tried it before, because I never had a girl I thought could do it. All along, though, I've had a reverse setup in mind—with a man doing the canvassing and a girl closing his leads. I've made up my mind that Della's the girl I want to try that stunt with."

The way he was looking at her, Della got the impression that this wasn't the only stunt that Hank would like to try. "The sample kit would be awfully heavy," Della said, protesting mildly. She didn't want the job; there wasn't any more money in it, just additional headaches. She could make as much just being a canvasser and not have to worry about selling. She added, hopefully, "Besides, I don't have a car."

"Well?"

"That kit weighs at least fifty pounds."

"Sixty-two," Charlie Short said. "With a jug of whiskey in it."

"I'll make all the arrangements for you," Hank told her, ignoring Charlie. He picked up the blackboard pointer, tapping it lightly on the table. "Besides, your canvasser will have a car and that'll be a way for you to get around and carry your things, too."

Della saw that this was something which she couldn't

avoid—at least, not at the moment.

"When do I start—closing?"

Hank shrugged. "Who knows? Tomorrow. Next week. Just as soon as Jack runs out of money and comes back to work."

"Holy!" Della breathed.

"Well, for gosh sake!" Len exploded, holding his hands wide, pleading with everybody. "Whoever heard of a thing like that? Jack's the best man in the office and we all know it."

"When he isn't drinking," Hank said.

"One man's vice," Charlie Short murmured, "is another man's—"

"Okay," Hank said. "Okay, Charlie. You keep it up and you'll wind up with a woman boss."

Charlie thought about that, rubbed his hands together and grinned.

"Gee, when do I start?"

Hank laughed and Billie leaned over and slapped Charlie across the back of the neck.

"Break it up, kiddies," Hank said. He looked at Della. "When we're finished here, come in the office and we'll talk things over."

"All right, Hank."

Hank turned his attention to the progress chart. He had his back to them, lifting the pointer to follow the rows of figures on the board. Len Parks and Charlie Short took advantage of the situation and started matching coins. Billie Norton kept staring at Della's legs, then down at her own. Jo Ann Hale sat idly buffing her fingernails.

No one paid very much heed to what Hank was saying. And no one, least of all Hank, expected anybody to listen. The meetings were required by the company—section eight, subdivision nine of the manual, entitled, Established Procedures for Wyandot Field Personnel—and that's all they amounted to.

Della heard Hank speak of quarter periods and quotas and business in the mill. None of it meant very much to her. She kept thinking about what a lousy thing Hank planned to do with her. Jack canvassing! And she doing the selling for him! Of course, Hank had no way of knowing that she had once shared a bed with Jack and that that might make a difference.

The meeting broke up around ten-thirty. Everybody was asking everybody else, at the same time, what the other was going to do that day. This being Friday and practically the end of the week, there were loud promises of working it out to the last sidewall that day, of finishing up a stinking week with a bang. Everybody was lying and everybody knew it. This was the end of the week, the day to loaf over coffee, to find a nice quiet bar and watch the ball game on television, to go home to the wife and kids, or to just go out and get drunk and get fixed up.

Della followed Hank into his small office. She left the door open, seeking some relief from the rising heat, but he came around his desk and closed it. Hank moved his big bulk into a small space behind the desk, shuffled a couple of papers and finally sat down in a rickety chair that threatened to collapse.

"Sit down, Della."

She sat down, crossing her legs. She took out a cigarette and lighted it. The smoke hovered in a little cloud between them.

"I guess I surprised you, Della."

He laughed. He had a friendly face, big and oval and somewhat on the red side. He had a strong face, except for his chin which was small, almost to the point of being babyish.

"You've been doing a good job, Della. Your leads have been good. You give the closer a fair chance, because you sell the need for the job yourself." He glanced down at the ink spotted blotter before him. "Maybe it's because you're beautiful—a kind of beauty that's hard for me to explain."

She met his long look full and direct. Was he making her an offer? His eyes told her nothing. Her eyes told him that, if he was, the price would be high.

"You've got the kind of beauty that takes a man over," he went on. "I'm not telling you anything new because you're the kind of a woman who knows it. In our business, your kind of beauty can be helpful—but it can also be a hindrance. Not properly used, your looks could put another woman on the defensive, if not arouse her utter dislike, especially if she thought you might be commercializing it."

The soft blue of Della's eyes became pouting and hurt. All of the virginity in all the world was written in that look for him to see. He saw and his face got a darker shade of red and he fumbled with the collar of his shirt.

"That was pretty crude of me, wasn't it?"

"I think I know what you meant, Hank."

"I didn't mean it as it sounded. I merely wanted to point out that you give the impression that you are the type of woman who might depend upon beauty alone. You have to watch out for that. It's fine to be beautiful but you have to get them thinking that you're saving it for one final, complete love."

Amen, Della thought.

"Now, I want to tell you what this proposition is I have in mind for you. As I said a little while ago, I had in mind trying a woman as a closer. But until you came along I hadn't found the right one. Do you follow me?"

"Not quite," Della said. Maybe now was the time to get off the hook. "I don't see how you can tell about me when I've been here such a short time."

"You've been here long enough."

"Two weeks."

"I don't have to have people around me very long before

I get to know them. I'm a pretty good judge of human character. Yours stands up, Della. You're solid for this business."

His eyes were now mentally measuring the distance around her breasts, whether or not she wore a girdle, if she were really blonde, if she did or she didn't.

"I've got a feeling, Della, that there's going to be a man-power shortage like there's never been before. Some of our men will be going into service, and some of them won't come back. This is the kind of work a woman can do, if she puts her mind to it."

"I don't know," she said. "It just seems to me that I'd be better prepared a month or ten months from now. Don't you?"

"Go on. There's something on your mind."

"That's all."

"No, it isn't."

"I've had fun doing this canvassing." Her smile played on him. "You know, talking to people, not knowing just what to expect at the next place, jockeying people into a position for an interview. I—well, right now I'm making just as much as the salesmen. And I don't have to sell the jobs."

Hank grinned. He offered her a cigarette, but she already had one and she shook her head.

"I figured that was what you were going to say. And how did I know? They're like records—they all say the same thing."

"It's true."

"Of course it's true. And they always become closers, Della." His voice was quietly firm. "Always. I never miss. People in this office do as I want them to do. To some," he said, more gently, "I offer inducements."

Her head tilted suspiciously.

"Such as?"

"Dammit!" he said. "I can never get used to sparring

words with a woman. I've got to get things right out in the open where I can see them." He leaned across the desk toward her.

"Look, mister," she told him, harshly, "if you've got anything to say, say it."

He laughed and straightened in his chair.

"Only beautiful women can afford to have tempers," he said. After a moment of thought, he went on, "First, I want you to work with Jack as his closer. You'll like that, won't you?"

"I'm quite certain that I'll hate every minute of it," Della said earnestly. "And so will Jack."

The heat of the morning grew oppressive in the small room. She wished that Hank had left the door open. "That's fine!" Hank told her. "Usually I have trouble with these girl-and-boy combinations. They always seem to want to be doing something that they can't get paid for. But if they don't like each other, or resent each other's presence, they get along swell, because all they want to do is their work and call it a day."

"Happy, happy family," Della said.

"Well, I don't think this is going to humiliate Jack in the least. He's a good salesman and he's been in this game long enough so that he'll take everything as just another busted shingle. But there's more to it than that."

Della's eyes narrowed.

"How much more?"

"You wouldn't know about this, Della, but every two years a Wyandot office must produce someone who is qualified to manage another territory. This is my year and I knew a long while ago that I'd have to recommend someone for the office in Bolton."

"And you recommended Jack?"

"You don't guess so good this morning, Della. No, I didn't give anybody's name, but I had Jack in mind. Jack sober I had in mind—Jack drunk I just forgot about.

You've seen what I've got here in the office. None of the old men would fit except Jack, so I've been hiring and firing men right and left, trying to grab onto a prospect that would show up for work every day. You see the last one I hired? He's a fairy if I ever saw one!"

"I just noticed his nail polish," she said.

"Yeah. Ain't he pretty?"

Della lit another cigarette and Hank reached for one. She handed him the pack.

"So, Hank, I work with Jack and we get as much business as we can. We knock ourselves out making a good showing."

"Right."

"And when everything is fine again you give him a promotion to Bolton?"

"How wrong can you be?"

"I don't know. You tell me."

"Very." He considered the tip of his cigarette. "You'll be the one who'll get the promotion, Della."

"Me?" she gasped.

"Yes, you! The first woman manager in Wyandot history. And you'll make a good one, Della. There isn't a woman who wouldn't be afraid of you, or a man who wouldn't do anything you asked."

Mounting excitement surged within her. A manager with Wyandot—that would be something! Lord, a manager made a lot of money every year. There were plenty of angles to the job which she didn't understand, but she had heard that a manager's annual take was almost fantastic.

"Of course, the promotion is only tentative, Della. It's just a promise on my part."

"Oh," she said, disappointed.

"All you have to do is have a record that I can sell them. That's all. You'll do it. With Jack's assistance, you'll knock their eyes out. I know it."

"How long would this be?"

"Not long," he assured her. "Just a matter of a few weeks."

She felt his stare racing along the contours of her body, halting and digging down there where the front of her dress was almost too low.

"Della, my promises are usually pretty good," he said. "I make them good."

She had heard around the office that there wasn't a favor too small for Hank to grant—or a price so high that he wouldn't ask it.

"You do what I want you to do," Hank told her, "and we won't have any trouble at all."

She pushed a curl away from her face, took a long drag on her cigarette and blew the smoke at the ceiling. Then she ran her tongue slowly across her lips and gave him a great big smile.

"We aren't going to have any trouble," she said, uncrossing her legs. "None at all, Hank."

Then she looked at his full bulk, took a deep breath and shuddered inwardly.

<h1 style="text-align:center">7</h1>

Della and Jack worked together every day during the following month, Saturdays included. They even worked a couple of Sunday mornings, out in the country, when they could talk to some of the people who had weekend homes there and lived and worked in New York most of the time.

He would pick her up at the office every morning with his car and they would start off, discussing the previous day's business, talking of old and new prospects, always planning how they could make today even better. Jack was principally interested in the money his efforts would bring, while Della had her sights set on the same thing—and something better for the day after tomorrow.

Her initial anxiety about working like this with Jack had soon faded. She found him courteous, friendly, helpful—and extremely subdued. Not once did he gripe about being the canvasser, nor had he mentioned that night in the hotel room, though she could tell from the way he often looked at her that it was very much on his mind.

Since that Friday in the office she had hardly seen Hank Annabella. Only once had he approached her, and that was to tell her, during the third week, what a swell job she was doing and that she must keep bearing down as the promotion was only around the corner of the next pile of shingles.

Her last weekly pay had been over three hundred dollars. She had opened a bank account and was having fun watching it grow. Only she wanted it to be bigger. Much bigger, with a lot of zeros on the end of it.

During their fifth week together Della and Jack hit their first dry spell. It had been heading their way for several days, born of too much confidence and past success. They had both seen it coming, but had not said much about it. Vainly, all that week they had fought it off, calling back on old clients, badgering everybody they talked to, getting a few little jobs here and there.

It was around five in the afternoon. They were returning from the nearby town of Collinsburg, driving through the quiet hills, the tires of the Buick roaring on the rough macadam.

"Well, Della," Jack said, "I guess you can say now that you've had it."

She shrugged. She was tired, very tired, and the thought of the week ending without any worthwhile business terrified her. She tried to think of someone they could slam a quick job at. The names whirred through her mind as though it were a machine sorting cards. Benson—no, he'd threatened to throw them off the porch. No wonder he'd acted like that, with the bitch of a wife he had. Snare? Hell, not that guy—he was too smart, knew all the answers and didn't have a dime to his name. Denning. Marks. Wilson.

"I guess we knocked on every damned door in that town," Della said, thinking about Collinsburg. "It wasn't as though the houses were nice and clean and didn't need any work. They were a mess, every last one of them. I can't understand it, Jack."

He took a while before he answered.

"No one understands it," he said. "Every salesman in every line, hits one of these weeks occasionally. I've had so many that I look forward to it. Why? Because I know that when I do come out of the slump, I'll have such a sharp edge that I'll be good enough to sell just about any-body I talk to."

Della laughed and threw her head back against the cush-ions. Her hair fell around her shoulders, the curls tight in the wind, framing the soft anxiety in her face.

"Jack," she said. "Jack, I wish that you'd get one of those feelings right now."

"Aw, don't worry about it!" He braked the car, barely missed a scurrying woodchuck. "I'm not going to worry about it. If they want to give me that promotion, okay; if they don't—they know what they can do with it."

She didn't say anything. She remembered that first day Jack had returned to work. He had been called into the inner office by Hank and he'd stayed in there a long time. From what Jack told her later, Della knew that Hank had given him the impression that this new arrangement was an attempt to swing the promotion for Jack. She hadn't talked very much about it.

"Do you really want this promotion?" she asked.

His foot eased up on the gas pedal.

"Maybe I do and maybe I don't. The money would be

all right, but there is a responsibility that goes with a job of that type that I'm not sure that I want. A manager can't put anything off until tomorrow. He's got to be on the ball all the time, never letting up. I can't quite see myself doing that. I like this wandering around from day to day, making my own plans, not having somebody riding herd on me all the time." He looked at her for a moment steadily, then winked. "Cowboy," he said.

She laughed and this time she meant it. He didn't want the job. He didn't give a damn about it. That made her feel good. When she got to be manager she had plans for Jack, a lot of them.

"How about your wife?" Della asked. "How does she feel about it?"

He was silent for a long moment.

"That slut!" he said finally, his lips hard.

His knuckles were white on the wheel, and he put his foot down harder on the gas.

"Sorry," he said. "But that's the way the ground's torn up. She likes anything that's got a dollar bill fastened to it. She even likes me if I've got money in my pocket— even better if my money happens to be in her own pocket. I'm telling you, it's no good."

"We've all got a yen for money," Della told him. "Some a little more than others maybe."

He drove on a short distance in silence.

"That just came out, Della. I didn't mean to talk about it. But I guess my nerves are a little ragged this week. I just get sore when I think about it. Hank Annabella and Shirley! Ain't that a laugh? That big slob!"

Della sat up quickly, thinking that this was about the craziest thing she'd ever heard. She didn't know what kind of a girl Shirley was—she'd only seen her once, a couple of Sundays before when the company had thrown its annual picnic—but she couldn't imagine any woman choosing Hank over Jack. Shirley had appeared to be dark and quiet, a little confused at the horsing around, but she remembered that Hank and Shirley had sung a few songs together. Hank was married, but Della hadn't ever thought of things being like this.

The car slowed, climbing a sharp incline, weaving around an abrupt curve in the road.

"I don't think anybody else in the office knows what I've just told you, Della." Jack's stare was full and hard. "If I were you, I wouldn't circulate the story."

"It's none of my business."

"That's what I mean." Then he said, viciously, "The bitch! The dirty bitch!"

"Please, Jack!"

"Why shouldn't I say it?" The pain was there in his voice and she knew that old wounds were running open. "Here I am, holding down a job just because of my wife's indiscretions. For what other reason do you think that Hank always takes me back? Because I'm so well qualified? Hell, no! It's because my wife is so well qualified!"

"What an awful thing to say!"

But, of course, Della thought no such thing. So Jack's wife liked variety, and maybe that was tough on Jack, but it was nothing to her. In fact, it could be helpful. It might mean that he would be just as satisfied to go to Bolton as her salesman as he would to go as manager. He was the kind of a guy, who, once led right, could be of tremendous help to her. He'd been in the business a long time; he knew the ropes and the knots that could be tied in them; it was a question of dangling something in front of him that would spur him on until he drove himself crazy writing business for her. She had an idea that she knew what she'd dangle. It was all right with her. She enjoyed it, too. Jack was a hell of a good lover.

"Maybe you're wrong about that," she offered. She had to be sure. And now was the time to find out, when he would think that she was being sympathetic and helpful.

"Wrong?" he asked bitterly. "No, because I saw them myself, once. Back there where the shingles are piled in the storage shed. It was at night and I'd come back to pick up some blank contracts. The headlights of my car—the car I had before this one, the one I wrecked—picked them up. I didn't stop. I never let on. I just drove on through the alley. But I can still see them—"

She shook her head sadly, but inside she laughed. He was cracking wide open and she could see the big split in the veneer that had surrounded him. She was no longer afraid of him. He was a man and she was a woman and she had him for as long as she had use for him.

"I've done this work a long while, Della—so long I'm actually afraid to try something else. I've got to the point where any legitimate sales work would throw me out of stride. Once I thought I wanted to be a farmer. It still thinks good. But that's all. Somehow, I can't change. I just go on, knowing what's happening, trying to lose myself in my work. Sometimes, when I go home and crawl in bed with Shirley I wonder if he's just left. And, sometimes, I lay there thinking about this promotion, wondering if it's true, wondering if she's bought it with the only thing that she has to pay him off with."

The wind ripped at Della's hair, and the fresh, clean smell of new-cut hay filled the air. It used to smell like that when the farmers made the second cutting along the Willowkill. She thought of her father and mother back there on the old place. She could almost hear her mother yelling at her father about cutting the grass on the lawn—"You want me to get bit by a snake, you old fool?"—and she could see her father whacking away at the tough wire grass with the old scythe he had to use because the lawn mower was busted and they'd never be able to afford another one.

She saw all that, and more, and she was glad she was away from it. She was glad that she was where she was, that Jack's wife was such a bitch, that Jack was such a fool, that everything was going to be all right.

On either side of the road stretched acres of black dirt fields, dotted with thousands of onion and lettuce plants. Here the people of Polish descent toiled in their fields from daylight to dark, drank cold beer in the stale smelling taverns at night, went to church on Sunday and prayed that the hand of God would protect their crops. They neglected the appearance of their homes and their buildings. Paint and shingles and a beautiful exterior meant nothing. All important was the lowly onion or lettuce plant, growing in the fields today, growing as dollars in the bank tomorrow.

"Jack!" Della cried excitedly. "Let's go over to that farm."

"Waste of time," he said wearily. "I've called on every one of these muckers, at one time or another. So had everybody else in the office. They'll buy television sets, deep freezes and big cars—but they won't resurface their houses until the shingles just naturally drop off."

"I want to go over there, anyway," she persisted, undismayed.

Jack shrugged and turned in at the next dirt lane. Della studied the house carefully. It was fairly large and badly weatherbeaten but it had a low gable. There was a lot of gingerbread work on it that ought to be knocked off, and that would give it some clean lines. About a thousand dollars would make it look like a new place. Just a lousy thousand bucks. Lord, if they could only get this job! If she could only hang on a few weeks more, producing as she had in the past, she'd be able to sit back and tell somebody else to go out and dig up the work.

"We're going to have this job!" she assured Jack. "If it's the last damn thing I ever do."

He grinned at her.

"When you talk like that, baby, heaven help them!"

An elderly couple was seated on the porch. The woman, short and fat in a long white house dress, sat in a rocking chair, banging a loose board on the floor as she pushed herself slowly back and forth. The man, equally short and with gnarled hands and gray hair, sat on the top step, busily pouring lemonade out of a cracked pitcher into two thick glasses.

Della walked to the porch. Jack followed, carrying the sample case of shingles. The old woman wrinkled her nose and stared into the sunlight at Della, her rocking chair now quiet. The man put the pitcher down and stood up.

"Hello!" Della said.

"Hello," the man replied doubtfully. The woman merely nodded.

"How's the onion business?" Della inquired. She went up onto the porch, slowly, giving him a good whiff of her perfume, and planted herself firmly on a bench that ran along the porch railing. Jack put the shingles on the ground and lit a cigarette. He gave the old woman a broad smile and she snickered back at him.

"Fine as ever," the man replied, speaking English surprisingly well. He came over and hitched himself up onto the railing, hooked his mud-caked shoes around a couple of spindles. "What do you want, miss?"

"Mr. Halbrgross?" It always helped to call them by their right name, and she had noticed that on the mailbox. He wagged his head and smiled down at her. "Well, we are with the Wyandot Roofing Company, and—"

Mr. Halbrgross looked angry. "Why do you people keep coming around here?" he demanded. He turned to his wife. "Minnie, ain't this about the tenth time somebody from that outfit's been here?"

"More'n that," the woman agreed, sourly. She started rocking again, all interest in her visitors apparently having vanished. "Every day they're here, seems like."

"Oh, I'm terribly sorry!" Della stood up, took a deep breath and let the old guy get a good look at her thirty-eight bust. "We didn't realize that one of our representatives had contacted you. We didn't mean to annoy you."

Mr. Halbrgross took another long look at her.

"That's all right," he said. "I'm not blaming you."

Della turned to Jack, her voice feigning disgust.

"Can you imagine that, Mr. Bishop? Letting us come all the way out here to bother these nice folks. I think it's a shame. Some of our people are just too lazy to fill out those forms."

"We'll report this to the boss."

"Indeed we will!" Della's smile, soft and begging forgiveness, appraised both Mr. and Mrs. Halbrgross. "Please, accept our apology."

Mr. Halbrgross moved enough so that he could take a dead sight at the hollow between Della's breasts.

"Oh, sure," he said.

"But, while we're here, there's just a couple of things I'd like to ask you folks. By doing so, I think we can save you a lot of unnecessary trouble from our people in the future."

"It really isn't such an awful lot of trouble," Mr. Halbrgross assured her, his eyes following the rise and fall of her dress.

"Well, it certainly is," his wife said, rocking a little faster.

"I'm sure Mrs. Halbrgross is right," Della said. The old bitch! "Now, did anyone ever give you a demonstration of our shingles?"

"For heaven's sake, yes! Why, I guess—"

"I just wanted to be sure, Mrs. Halbrgross."

"Several times," her husband said.

"Well, fine. I mean, it's fine for you but not for us. You see Mr. Halbrgross, we're just talkers for the company. That is, we go around and talk to people and show them what we have. Then if the people want anything they just come into the office and ask for it. The company thinks this is a better way of advertising, rather than going on the radio or taking ads in the-papers."

"You can shut off a radio," Mrs. Halbrgross said.

Della favored her with a sweet smile, but the old lady was having none of it.

"We only get paid by the calls we make. That's why I can't understand why the other people who were here didn't take care of it. The company requires us to fill out a form, to support our pay voucher, stating the name of the owners we talked to, a description of the property and any pertinent things like that. Of course, some people are so mean to us that they won't let us do it."

"I don't know what gets into some people," Mr. Halbrgross said, shaking his head. "I sure don't."

"The forms are numbered, so that we can't waste them," Della went on, leading him further into the trap. "I want to be sure that you haven't filled out one before I do so myself and get in trouble."

The man looked at his wife.

"No one ever did that here, did they, Minnie?"

"I don't think so," Della put in hastily. "If they had, why—"

"Well, for mercy's sakes fill it out!" Mrs. Halbrgross shouted urgently. The front of Della's dress had dropped another half an inch and the old lady was developing a clear case of anxiety. She had just caught up with her husband's glowering stare, and now she directed her wrath at him. "Waldo, if you let any more of these people in here, with forms and all that stuff, I'll kick your back side!"

"Minnie!"

"I said I would kick your back side, Waldo Halbrgross!" She started rocking again and the loose board thumped good and loud. "I'm meanin' it, too!"

"Jack," Della said, hardly able to restrain her laughter.

"The forms, if you please. The blue ones."

He handed her the book of applications, his eyes dark and thoughtful. Della checked to make sure the carbons were in order and then coolly started asking the necessary questions. Their names? Waldo B. and Minnie. How long had they lived there? He said ten years and she said twelve. And a brief description of the property. Those were all the questions which she asked. A couple of other things, such as the amount of their annual income and whether or not there was a mortgage on the place, she skipped over as not being practical at the moment. Besides, the retail credit report always dug up that kind of information.

"Well," she said finally, "I guess that does it. Except that I have to get you to sign."

"Sign?" Mrs. Halbrgross demanded. "Not by a damned sight!"

"Oh, please!" Della begged her. "Please, Mrs. Halbrgross, we've spent so much time here and we've tried to help you and we won't get paid unless you do."

"Why not?"

"The company wouldn't have any proof that we'd been here. We won't get paid unless you give us—a break. Please, won't you?"

"I'll sign it," Mr. Halbrgross said.

Della stood close to him and held the pad steady. He made believe he was reading the form, but he was looking some place else. He signed his name in a careless scrawl.

"Now, you sign it, Minnie," he told his wife, his voice a trifle sharp.

Mrs. Halbrgross' signature was small and backhand and Della had quite a bit of trouble getting her to see which was the proper line.

"Well, that settles your troubles," Della assured them, handing the pad to Jack. "I won't be back again."

If they thought—or old man Halbrgross hoped—that she'd ever show herself around there again, they were nuts. She had all she wanted from them. She could get plenty of fancy stares and cold looks some place else.

She said good-bye to Mrs. Halbrgross, gave the old guy a farewell shake of her hips and followed Jack out to the car. She trembled a little, getting into the car, as she thought about what she had done. Then she consoled herself with the fact that it wasn't any worse than some of the things that others in the office pulled. Not much worse, anyway.

Jack drove the car slowly down the bumpy lane, turned left at the highway and picked up speed. The smell of crushed onion tops filled the air and bit at Della's nostrils. The sun blinked through the trees of a faraway hill and occasional patches of gathering dusk stretched giant fingers across the surface of the road.

"You know something, Della?"

"No."

"That was about the rawest stunt I've ever seen pulled."

"Oh, come now," she pleaded, leaning her body close to him. "You're not going moral on me, are you?"

"Know any more good jokes?"

"Not any as funny."

"I'm worried about you," he said, and let out a low whistle. "Is there anything that you wouldn't do, Della?"

"Now don't try to spoil it," she warned him. She took a full breath and leaned back into the cushions. "Wasn't it wonderful? Those dummies!"

"Yeah." He laughed and put his arm around her, "You can say that again."

She felt very close to Jack at this moment, sharing this larceny with him. She felt again almost like she had felt that night in the hotel room, only now it was the whole world that was small and there was just the two of them, no one else, and if there had been it would not have mattered.

Down the road there was a tourist court, its neon sign blinking through the growing darkness.

It took them until the next morning to drive the remaining five miles to town.

8

Summer died into the brown of the leaves on the trees, the yellowed grass on the lawns, the chill winds of October. Summer died and with it passed another quarter in the progress chart of the Wyandot Roofing Company.

Della had now moved into an apartment of her own, a little three room affair in a neighborhood of high rents where nobody cared very much about what the other person did. She had a kitchen, though she used this compact space more for fixing highballs than she did for cooking. The living room was large with plenty of windows and venetian blinds, a thick gray rug, a big roomy davenport, a couple of easy chairs, a desk with a trick ink well and a fistful of lamps. There was also a fireplace that burned gas and smelled like hell.

At the moment she lay on the big bed in the bedroom, wearing a pair of thirty-five dollar pajamas, listening to the radio that told of peace in Korea, of a single movie actress who was adopting a kid because she'd never had time to get fixed up—or couldn't—of a new increase in taxes that would knock her salary for a loop. She laughed at the radio and shut it off. She was smart. She'd sent her father and mother some money and she'd declared them as dependents. It was cheaper to keep them than it was to ignore them.

"Damn!" she said and sat up.

She looked for her cigarettes, but there weren't any on the table and she was too tired to bother getting them out of her coat. What a hell of a way to feel on Saturday night! What a hell of a way in which to spend a weekend! Alone. She was like a machine that has gone at top speed all week and now waited only for Monday morning and the chance to get under way again.

She laughed. It had been worth it. Not much fun, but worth every frantic moment of it. That night in the tourist cabin with Jack she had decided that there would be no more of that—not, at least, until she reached the point where she no longer gave a hoot in hell about him. Liking a man too much could be disastrous, especially if a woman planned on using him. And she was going to use Jack. For all he was worth, and then some.

It had been tough. She had lost weight. Not around her hips—they were still thirty-six and put a lot of strain on her clothes when she walked. No, she'd lost it around the waist, which was down to twenty-four now and that made her breasts look bigger, and the men stare longer. That was all right, as long as she never got too big down there. If that ever happened, she didn't know what she'd do about it.

Della shuddered and stood up, the soft line of the pajamas pressing in all around her. So what if she had worked her head off? Hadn't it been worth it? Her bank account said so, Hank Annabella said so and everybody in the office, including the doubtful Miss Johnson, said so. That should be enough for anybody.

The Halbrgross deal had opened up a new world to her, a world of selling by coercion, lies, threats—anything short of using a club or a gun. Even Hank Annabella had been amazed at Della's blank admission of the facts surrounding the Halbrgross swindle. But he had listened to her, followed her instructions and the whole thing had run off like water sliding down a Wyandot shingle.

Joe Adams, the truck driver, had been dubious at first, but he had followed through for her on the promise of a twenty. There had been three other shingle jobs loaded on the huge truck and she had had the material for the Halbrgross place stuck on the rear. Of course, the old couple had raised a hell of a rumpus when Joe got out there to their place and tried to park the stuff in their front yard. They'd told Joe that they hadn't ordered any shingles, they didn't need any shingles, and, by cripes, they weren't having any.

Joe had recited his lines, saying that he didn't know anything about it, that he was just a poor slob driving a truck for a living. Then Joe explained to Mr. and Mrs. Halbrgross that he had three other jobs on the truck, with theirs on the rear, and if he couldn't leave their part of the load some place he'd have to take it off and put it back on again every place he stopped. Mr. Halbrgross pointed out that Joe could take the shingles back to the warehouse before he went any farther and then Joe's troubles would be over. But Joe had screwed up this thin, sad face and told them that the boss was as cranky as all hell early in the morning, and he might get fired if he went back now, but that it would be okay if he returned the stuff late in the afternoon when the boss was in a good mood.

Joe told them that he had a sick kid in the hospital— this happened to be true—and he couldn't afford to take a chance with his job. The only thing he asked was for Mr. Halbrgross to let him leave the shingles there in the front yard and he'd pick them up later that day.

Mr. Halbrgross had cursed Wyandot roundly and helped Joe unload the shingles.

Quite naturally, Joe Adams never got back to their place that day.

The next morning after that Della planned her next move. By this time Hank Annabella was beginning to learn something new about the roofing and robbing business, so he'd kept his mouth shut and listened.

The two carpenters whom she had dispatched to the scene of her finagling, called on the phone about ten that morning to tell Della that Mr. Halbrgross was showing a great deal of resistance.

"Just walk up to the house and nail on a couple of shingles," she'd told Mike crisply. "Then forget about it. The contract'll be in force after that."

"Holy Mother!" Mike had exploded. "I want to forget about it right now. Gee, Miss Banners, the old guy's out there in his yard with a shotgun. The way his old woman's yelling at him, he's apt to do almost anything."

"He can go to hell," Della had said.

Mike had been silent for a moment.

"Maybe you should come down here and tell him that, Miss Banners. Sure, I don't want to have the honor. He'll have me lookin' like a sieve."

Thinking about it now, and especially the way it had turned out, it seemed pretty funny to Della.

She'd borrowed Jack's car and driven out there to the farm. Mr. Halbrgross had been out in his yard all right, shotgun in the crook of his arm, angry eyes squinting into the sun. Mrs. Halbrgross had been on the porch reviewing her husband's history in no uncertain terms, none of which were meant to be complimentary. The two carpenters sat out front in their pick-up truck, ready to leave the scene without any encouragement at all.

Della wondered just what she would have done if Mr. Halbrgross hadn't called the state police just before her arrival. She supposed that she might have apologized to the old couple, had the company remove the shingles from their premises, cried and quit the siding racket—or simply compromised and gone to bed with Hank Annabella.

As it turned out, the police arrived while she was gingerly stepping from the car. Mr. Halbrgross had come out to the road and shouted at Della and the troopers at the same time. The old woman had come down off the porch, limping and screaming her lungs out. It had been the big, dark-haired trooper with the black mustache who had unknowingly come to Della's rescue.

"Peace," he had said, grinning, "it's wonderful. Let's have some. Maybe, then, I can figure out whether this is an assault case or just a camp meeting out of hand."

There had been a hushed silence, but the tension had started mounting as soon as the trooper began asking questions. Yes, he understood that Mr. Halbrgross didn't want the shingles on his house. That was quite evident. Now, had Mr. Halbrgross signed any kind of a paper? Well, yes, he had. And did the pretty young lady, standing there, have the paper with her? Of course. The trooper had glanced at the copy of the contract and then asked Mr. and Mrs. Halbrgross if they had signed it. Yes, they had, because the lady had said—

"I don't know what the lady said," the trooper had broken in. "That isn't my business, any more than it's my job to go around telling people what they should or should not sign. But after you've signed something, like you folks have, it becomes my job to tell you what you have to do. You people signed a contract to have shingles applied to your home by the Wyandot Roofing Company. The company has delivered the necessary material to your place, and the workmen are here to do the job. If you interfere with these men while they are completing the company's part of the contract, you will be in violation of the law."

Period, thought Della. One great big, beautiful, damned period!

The end of the Halbrgross affair, as she liked to think of it, had come a couple of weeks later when the old couple had walked into the office and slapped down a check in full payment for the job. They were apologetic. They just loved the appearance of their home! It was beautiful! And so many of their neighbors were complimentary and jealous of it at the same time. Most of the other people around the black dirt section would like some kind of work done on their places. Perhaps, when Della wasn't too busy, she'd have time to stop around and see some of those folks.

Della yawned sleepily and lay down again, pressing deep into the softness of the bed. She was sick of onion farmers and shingles and contracts. She was weary of business, business and more business. Sure, it was nice on payday and this apartment was nice, but her whole existence was so lonely. Work, plan and sleep alone. Go to bed early on Saturday night and sleep all day Sunday so that she could charge up her batteries for a quick start Monday morning. How very interesting!

She got up again and walked over to the window. She heard the baby next door crying and she wondered what the father and mother were doing. She laughed. She'd tried playing house with them before, speculating about what went on over there, and she always came up with the same answer.

Outside the wind lashed at the dry leaves still hanging on the maples. The electric light and telephone wires bounced up and down like streamers over a hot air register. A man and woman crossed the street, their bodies close, their heads bent against the bite of the wind. A dog came out of the shadows, barked a couple of times and disappeared.

She turned away from the window. Hank had told her that morning that her promotion might come any day now, just as soon as one of the big shots hit town and got sober enough to make a decision. Hank had forwarded his recommendation and her record had backed up every good thing he'd said about her. She wondered what it would be like. She had worked and fought and lied to qualify for the chance as a branch manager. It had better be good, mighty good.

At that precise moment, Della Banners felt like hell.

She wandered aimlessly around the room. Her hair was longer now, farther down on her shoulders, almost softer, giving her face a deep, sincere glow. She hesitated, picked up the phone and dialed a number. But she put it down before anyone could answer. Every day of every week she had struggled and won over this feeling. He didn't have a thing to offer her except his body and that wasn't enough. Or could that be the trouble? Was she so stupid that she was beginning to think that it was enough?

She went out into the living room. She wasn't going to sit around and think about it. If, for biological reasons, she needed a man, she could always find one who wouldn't have to mean anything to her afterward. Maybe a movie would help. Or a drink of Old Forester and a chaser of beer. Lord, how could people drink those combinations? Perhaps, though, if she just called Jack, just talked with him a few minutes, maybe about what they'd do Monday, or—

The door buzzer sounded. She picked up her robe from a chair, put it on and closed it tight and tied a huge bow. She wondered who it might be. Jack had never been up to the apartment and he'd only hinted at it once, the night he'd tried to get at her in the car and she'd rapped him one across the face. Hank Annabella had been up there one morning, around four, so drunk that he'd slept in the bathtub. She'd gotten him up the next morning by the simple expedient of turning on the cold water tap. She hoped that he wasn't returning for a curtain call on that one.

She flung the door open, then started to close it.

"Hello, Della."

"Well—Roy."

He stood there, tall and straight, looking very much out of place in his neat blue suit, white shirt and red tie. "I had a little trouble finding this place."

Not enough, she thought. Not nearly enough.

"I'd like to talk to you for a couple of minutes," he said.

She opened up the door again and he came sauntering

in. She didn't feel at all good about it. Roy was something out of her past, someone she had left parked alongside the Willowkill a long while ago. She hadn't realized until this moment how far she had gone since that day she'd driven past the bank in Harris. It was just a little frightening.

She closed the door, slowly, keenly aware of the fact that he had hardly looked at her. This annoyed her, because she knew that the robe fit tight and had some interesting angles.

"I've got some bad news for you, Della."

As far as she was concerned his coming, in itself, had been enough bad news.

"Your father is pretty sick, Della."

"Oh?" Somehow she wasn't surprised. "What's wrong with him?"

Roy shook his head and loosened his collar. She remembered that Roy never liked to have his shirt buttoned, but the top open, exposing the strong lines of his thick, brown throat. She looked away from his face, down at his hands, and she could see the traces of black grease that he had been unable to wash away.

"I don't know what's wrong with him," Roy said. "They've had a doctor for him, but he doesn't know what it is. Doc Martin told your mother that they ought to call in someone else."

Della could recall the time, during her high school days, when Doc Martin had been one of the town's drunkards. The death of a patient, because Doc had driven off the road in a drunken stupor and fallen asleep on the way to make the call, had permanently sobered him. After that Doc had taken good care of his patients, working around the clock as a sort of personal punishment for his past misdeeds.

"Well, I didn't know about that," Della said.

"He's flat down in bed, Della. Your mother's had quite

a time of it, taking care of him and doing everything else. She got a lift into town to go and get your check cashed and she stopped in at the station on her way home. She said she had your address, at last, and that she ought to write to you about your father. But she said she didn't know just what to say."

"I never expected her to write," Della said. "Unless it was for more money."

A touch of pain shot across Roy's face.

"I don't know anything about that, Della. Maybe you're right feeling as you do about some things, and maybe she is. I don't know. I just told your mother that maybe I could come down here and see you, tell you how things are. She was dead set against it. She'd be pretty mad, if she knew I was here."

Della went over and sat down in the deepness of the davenport. Roy looked at her uncertainly for a moment, then came over and sat down carefully at the other end of it. "Why should she be mad?"

"Well, she said that you just walked off and left them."

"I certainly did," Della agreed. "I was sick and tired of the damned place."

"And she said you could stay gone."

"Well, thanks," Della said. She lit a cigarette, taking her time about it, and then she told him, her voice brittle and lashing. "Look, mister, you came down here to give me a message and I guess you've done it. Now that you've made your little speech, stuck your barb into me, you can go."

The color drained from his face.

"Gosh, Della, you've got me all wrong. I just thought that you'd want to know. And there's something else, too. I know that your mother is pressed for money. This doctor coming every day—"

"I'd like to know a time when she wasn't pressed for money."

He shook his head.

"This is something different, Della. Your dad is really sick. I was up to see him—day before yesterday. Your father's got some money coming, but there's a hold-up on it. He said that the insurance man had been out to see him a couple of times, having him sign forms, but that this accident and health insurance company—"

"Oh, my lord!"

"What's so funny?"

Now she was laughing, low and soft. For a moment she had been worried. Actually, she had always been very fond of her father and she had cried inwardly at the thought that he might be ill.

"Don't you see, Roy? But, no, maybe you couldn't—not knowing him like I do. That's probably the real reason Mom didn't want you coming down here worrying me about something that isn't even there. Hell, I can see it all right now. My dad's always been tired of working—Mom says that he was born that way—but he'd never been able to figure out how he could stop completely. Then probably someone came along, selling sickness insurance, and he would be quick to see that he might be able to work that racket for a while."

"I heard that he might not get paid by the company," Roy said, crossing his legs. "Something about not having the policy long enough."

"He'll get well in a hurry," Della prophesied. "The day after they turn down his claim he'll be out fishing or hunting rabbits."

She got up and went over to the desk. The dressing gown was plastered to her curves and she could feel him watching her.

"Still beautiful," he said. "You've always been beautiful, Della."

"Thanks," she said. She knew damned well he was remembering that interlude along the Willowkill, trying to figure out how he could experience it again.

Roy stood up, glanced around the room and shifted his weight uncomfortably.

"I think you're wrong about your dad. I don't think he's down on his back for the reason you say. And I'm sure your mother doesn't feel that way about it either. He's a sick man, Della."

"All right, Doctor."

"I'm serious."

She picked up her checkbook and slapped it on the desk.

"So am I, Roy. You say he's sick, and I don't think so. So what do you want me to do? Send him flowers? He hates them."

Roy looked away from her, at the darkened window, toward the lights of the city beyond.

"I'm going to give you a check to take along with you, Roy. I'll make it out for five hundred. When he fastens his eyes on that he'll climb out of bed like the house is on fire."

"You're so wrong," Roy insisted, looking away from the window, his eyes pleading with her. "You don't know what you're saying. I didn't come down here to ask you for money for your parents. You're old enough to know whether you should send it to them, or you shouldn't. The only reason I came was to tell you about him and to ask you to go back up there with me."

"Oh?"

"I know he'd appreciate it, Della. You can give him the check yourself, if you want. The main thing is for you to see him."

She put the checkbook back on the desk. She stood there staring down at her blue slippers, and she could see him moving slowly across the room toward her.

"I'd like to have you come back with me for good," Roy said in a rush, his voice earnest. "I love you, Della. But that can wait. This is something else. This is something more important right now. But all of it's up to you."

Something deep inside her rolled around and dropped and cracked. She could smell the fog again and the thick of the willows along the stream and she could feel his hands there, wanting her—the first time that hands had been gentle and loving—and it made her disgusted because he should have said it then. He should have told her, holding her close and naked in the back seat of the car, that he loved her, not waiting until now when everything was so changed, when it was the only thing that he could say that might bring her to him again—when she no longer cared.

"If I thought he was really sick," Della murmured, "I'd go in a minute, but—"

"Then you'd better get dressed right now."

Maybe Roy wasn't telling her the truth. It might only be a trick to get her alone with him. But he wouldn't lie about a thing like that. Hardly. And she had been alone with him for several minutes now and they were almost like two strangers bumping into each other at a ticket counter.

"All right, Roy."

Going up with him tonight would give her a full day with her folks tomorrow—she could stand that!—and she could catch a bus back early Sunday evening.

Roy smiled at her for the first time since his arrival. "Good girl! I'll wait downstairs for you."

"I'll only be a few minutes."

"Sure."

At the door he turned and looked at the room again.

"I guess you're doing pretty good in your job?"

She nodded.

"I guess you must like it."

She started to say something when the telephone began screaming. Some day, Della decided, she'd get one of those buzzers that purred softly like a sleeping cat.

She knew who it was as soon as she picked up the phone and heard the voice.

"Hi, Hank!"

"Hello, Della."

Hank sounded a little bit drunk, but that didn't surprise her. Hank reserved his drinking for weekends only, but in those couple of days he'd drink almost as much as most men could put away in a month.

"Listen, Della, big things are breaking for you. Mr. Gordon is down here until tomorrow night."

"Who's Mr. Gordon?"

"A vice president of Wyandot. I've been talking to him about you taking the Bolton office. In fact, that's why he's here now."

"Oh, swell!"

Hank grunted.

"Up to this point it talks and listens good. But this Gordon, he's sort of tough. He's been all over your production record and that part is okay. Only he objects to a woman running an office. He says it's too much of a job for a woman. But, of course, he hasn't seen you yet, Della. When he gets his lamps fastened on you I know it'll be a different story."

"But he's going back tomorrow night, isn't he? That's Sunday."

"That's why I called you. We're having a little party for him down here at his hotel. We've been under way quite a spell now. He's pretty talkative now and in a mellow mood, so I sneaked down to the lobby to give you a ring. I want you to hop over here right away and nail this thing down for yourself. Okay, Della?"

Della glanced at Roy, waiting there by the door, and thought about her father only briefly. She knew very well that Roy didn't know what he was talking about. There wasn't anything wrong with Chuck Banners that an easy buck wouldn't cure in a hurry.

"Okay," she told Hank. "As soon as I can get some things on."

He told her not to put on too much, gave her the room number in the Kelly Hotel and hung up.

Della got out her checkbook again, found a pen with a scratchy point and scribbled a check to her father in the amount of five hundred dollars. Then she folded the check in the palm of her hand and took it over to Roy.

"Here," she said. "Give this to the old man and see if that doesn't bring him out of the bends."

"You—aren't going?"

"I'm not."

"But I thought you said—"

"For Pete's sake, forget what I said!" She flung herself toward the bedroom door. She didn't have any time to throw away. She wanted to get right down there and collar old man Gordon while he was still sober. She wanted that manager's job like she had never wanted anything else in her life before.

"What kind of a person are you?" Roy demanded, his voice angry. "Your own father sick and—"

She slammed the bedroom door closed, shutting out the noise.

9

The party which was in progress in Room 404 of the Kelly Hotel seemed to have been planned with the sole objective of testing the strength of the fifty year old structure. About twenty people were present in the two room suite, all in various stages of intoxication. A few managed to stay upright and dance to the weary music that cried slow and soft from the juke box which had been provided by the janitor who would, come morning, swear up hill and across the valley that he couldn't understand how the thing got up from the cellar.

Bottles of assorted colors and sizes, varying in contents from full to empty, were scattered around the two rooms as though there had been a minor explosion.

Following the entrance of Della Banners into this tangle of human bodies, a two minute silence was observed. During this interval the women who were present focused their bleary eyes upon this shimmering vision in blue, observed a common enemy and gave her the Big Stare. The men also stared, but in a different way—a way that left no doubts at all about what was on their minds.

"Good evening, everybody," Della breathed.

The blue dress clung to her body with the grace of a silken glove, billowing down from the waist around her brown, slim legs. Her arms were bare to her smooth, white shoulders and her breasts looked about to fight their way through the thin material. The curve of her red lips, moist and sensuous, parted and her teeth flashed white and even. Her hair hung in long waves, molding her face in a halo of calm serenity.

A Park Avenue call girl at the start of her nightly rounds had never looked better.

"Della!"

Hank came over to her, waddling, his flushed face beaming stupid approval. His green sport shirt was almost soaking wet across his full middle. Della wondered, vaguely, why so many fat men perspired around their bellies.

Following Hank was a gray haired man of medium height, only a couple of inches taller than Della. His shoulders were very square in a severe blue suit. He had a serious face, an outdoor face that could lie ten years off his age any day. His mouth was a thin, tight line, seemingly slashed across his face for the sole purpose of talking. His eyes, Della noted, were light blue, and she could read nothing in them as they gave her a good going over.

"Della, I want you to meet Roger Gordon." Hank's breath smelled of high class gin. "Roger, I want you to know one of the best salesmen we've ever had—a girl who has just about everything. Della Banners, Roger."

Roger Gordon chuckled and the blue in his eyes became very warm.

"Hank has only two faults, Della. He overestimates what he can do in business. And—" he paused for a moment, still looking at her—"he always underdescribes the beauty of a woman."

Della supposed that she was meant to blush, so she did. Mr. Gordon tried to keep his attention on her face, but she could see that he was having extreme difficulty.

"This is indeed a pleasure," Della told Mr. Gordon, placing just the proper amount of awe in her voice. She had an idea that it wasn't going to be any pleasure, just a lot of work, but the line sounded good.

Somebody fed the juke box another record and most of the other people started dancing again.

"You may be disappointed with me, Della," Mr. Gordon said, grinning weakly, fighting to get away from the hook that she had ready for him. "I have a habit of being all business."

Della sighed. He was starting to match wits with her already. Why didn't he just come out and say that he liked what he saw, that he was interested, but that he just wasn't sure how he ought to play at it? Why? That was a stupid question for her to ask of herself. Hell, he was a man, wasn't he?

"If you like your business—as I do, Mr. Gordon—that can sometimes be fun, too."

Hank's look thanked her for a minor victory. Mr. Gordon registered a faint smile and looked about uncomfortably. Jo Ann, staggering a little under an alcoholic load, left the room in company with the new salesman who wore fingernail polish and who had lately, it was reliably reported, taken to having his hair waved. Billie Norton was huddled on a davenport, deep in the shadows of the room, with Len Parks. It was impossible to tell what they were doing, but from their slow looks and laughter it was easy enough to tell what was on their minds.

"This is quite a blast Hank's got under way," Mr. Gordon said. "Does he do this all the time?"

"Not that I know of," Della said.

"You and Jack didn't check in at the office last night," Hank told her. "Everybody else did." He looked at Mr. Gordon. "When I told them that you were due in late in the evening, we decided to give you a little welcome. Then when you didn't show we just kept going and it turned into this rat race. Too bad you couldn't get here last night, Roger old boy, old boy."

"Heaven forbid!" Mr. Gordon said. He took Della gently by the arm. "Perhaps you'd like to have a little drink first, and later we can talk."

Della looked him over again, thoroughly this time. He appeared to be a tough piece of man. Talking—only talking—would suit her just fine.

"Great idea!" she said with enthusiasm.

They managed to cross the room without getting knocked down. She saw Charlie Short, slightly drunker than usual, looking through a bunch of empty glasses on a tray, probably hunting up one for the road. Annie Bolton was dancing with her plumber friend, cuddled up close, her slim body doggedly trying to follow her partner's stumbling steps.

"Rye or Scotch?" Mr. Gordon inquired, studying the bottles on the table. "Or a Tom Collins? That's always cooling."

"Beer," Della said, noting the dark pint bottles floating in a small tub of ice and water.

"Oh, please, not beer! That'll make you fat." She patted her slim middle.

"That won't make me fat," she said. His glance went down there and lingered. "Besides, I like beer."

"Well, all right."

She hated beer, but it never made her drunk, or sick, and that's why she preferred it. Rye or Scotch or any kind of whiskey usually put her emotions in high gear and she wasn't having any of that while fooling around with a Wyandot vice president.

He got one of the beer bottles out of the water and wiped it off with a towel. The opener slipped off the cap several times and when he did manage to get the bottle open, half the contents shot like a geyser toward the ceiling.

"Double dammit!" he said. "That's what I hate about beer."

"You must have shook it."

"Maybe I did." He poured some into a glass and handed it to her. "Some of it got on your dress."

"That's all right."

They lifted their glasses and clinked. His eyes bored through the smoke at her, and the corners of his mouth twisted in a smile.

"Luck, Della."

He drank his whiskey straight and he put it away with a flick of his wrist. Before she had finished taking a sip of the beer he was pouring himself another jolt of Old Grandad.

"I never drink when I'm working," he said, letting go with the second one.

"That's a good policy."

"You have to be on your toes in this business," Roger Gordon told her. He gave her a wink. "I guess you know that."

"I guess I do."

"You've run up an impressive record, Della. Everybody at the home office is talking about it."

"Well, thanks."

"How about another beer? Try not to make a mess of this one."

"This place is a wreck, anyway."

He pried the cap off another bottle and the beer foamed over the top and down across his hand.

"It sure is a wreck." This time he poured his own drink, straight again, into a water tumbler. He spilled a little of it as he handed her the beer. "Here's to shingles."

"Nail them up!" she said, knowing that he was feeling the drinks, glad that he was getting his ear on edge.

The noise in the room had grown in intensity. Someone had turned up the volume of the juke box and now a jitterbug record was blaring, wild and tinny. The walls vibrated with the thud of heavy feet. Jo Ann swung around fast, lifting her skirts high.

"We can't do much talking in here," Roger Gordon said, shouting to make himself heard. He put his head down alongside Della's face and spoke into her ear. "Perhaps it would be better if we went to my room."

Della had thought that she was already in his room, but of course that really didn't matter one way or another. She shrugged and finished her beer.

"I'll take along another bottle for you," he said.

"No."

"Then I'll bring this jug of Grandad along. Maybe you'll change your mind."

She followed him along one side of the room. He almost dropped the bottle getting the door open but he finally managed it and they went out into the hall. He went down to 408 and unlocked the door, setting the bottle down on the floor while he did so.

"Oh, you've got it," he said, reaching for the bottle.

"I've got it," she said.

They went in and he closed the door. It was a large room with two single beds. The ceiling light burned warm and yellow. The sounds from the party seeped through the plaster walls. The breath of a breeze mumbled through the partly opened window, rapped at the shade, then died into silence.

Roger Gordon went over to the nightstand between the beds, picked up the phone and put it down without speaking to the operator.

"I don't know," he said, watching Della as she set the bottle of Old Grandad on the dresser. "I was going to call home, but I guess I'll do it later."

He went into the bathroom and returned with two glasses. A little later, Della thought, and he'd be in such shape that he wouldn't give a damn about home. He came over to the dresser, got the bottle and carried it back to the bathroom.

"Want one?" he called to her.

She inspected her face in the mirror and gave herself an approving wink.

"Not too big," she said. "With water."

Her face looked in good condition, no lipstick smear or anything like that; but she wished she'd worn a brassiere. No wonder everybody out there in the room had stared at her.

She saw Roger Gordon come out of the bathroom, a glass in either hand. He stopped and stared at her.

"You're a pretty lovely creature," he said, weaving a trifle as he walked toward her.

"I haven't got a quarter with me, Mr. Gordon."

"You might try calling me Roger."

"That's easier," she agreed.

He coughed and handed her the glass.

"Hank's been telling me what a wonderful job you've been doing. He didn't have to tell me that. I knew. But one thing that I didn't expect was for him to pick you for the promotion to Bolton."

"No?" She took a taste of her drink, staring at him over

the rim of her glass. "How so?"

"Oh, I don't know. I guess a woman could do the job all right. But I think she would have a lot to overcome. It's never been done in the company. It's something that's never come up before. There's no precedent for it."

"Precedents," Della said, "are established by people doing things for the first time."

He finished his drink and regarded her thoughtfully. He lost his vice president's smile and gave her his little-boy-out-for-a-good-time grin.

"I can see now why you've been so successful," he told her. "You sort of put it on the line."

She gave him a lingering look and turned and walked over to the window. Her body was long and graceful and she didn't try to stop anything from moving.

"Who makes the managerial appointments, Roger?"

"I do," he said. "I'm in charge of personnel."

She heard him go into the bathroom again, listened to the gurgle of Old Grandad jumping into his glass.

"You admit that my record is—satisfactory?"

"You know that," he said, coming back and standing very close to her.

"Are you prejudiced against me?"

She saw one hand come around her and place the drink on the windowsill. Then he put his hands on her shoulders and turned her, very slowly, to face him.

"I'm afraid," he said, blinking his eyes so that they would focus right, "that my feelings might be just the opposite."

She gave him a silent, long-lashes-on-cheek treatment. She heard his labored breathing. His hand came up under her chin and forced her head roughly back. She opened her eyes full at him and tried to pull herself away—but not too hard.

"And just what is your opinion of me, Roger?"

She moved her shoulders slightly and the dress slid down

some more, halting just as it threatened to slip off her body. Her lips parted in a smile, full and warm and promising. Her eyes were anxious, imploring.

"You've got a way with men," he said. "That could be a big help to you in your job. But—really, I don't know just what to say, Della."

Holy damn, she thought, why doesn't he stop hedging? If he's such a big wheel, why doesn't he act like one? He had something that she wanted. If she happened to have something that he wanted, maybe they could make a trade.

"I've worked like a slave," she said, letting her voice tremble just enough. "Hank promised me so much and I believed him. I've been out in the field morning and night, Saturday and Sunday, just—"

She stopped talking. She was very close to Roger Gordon now, so close that he must see the naked outlines of her breasts beneath the dress, the dark nipples which weren't quite concealed by the sewed-on flowers. She let him see her like that for only a moment. She turned away quickly, facing the window again.

"Men are so stupid!" she told him, looking out into the night. "There are so many things that a woman can do."

"I know what you're doing to me," Roger Gordon said helplessly. "You're driving me nuts." She hadn't heard him walk across the room, but now the noise of a bedspring came to her. "Honest to heaven! I have to give this just—a little—thought."

She stood there at the window. Down on the street the neon lights swung back and forth in the rising wind that cried around the corner of the hotel. A guy came out of the restaurant across the street, got into his car, got out again and went, head bent against the wind, to the liquor store on the corner. The sounds of Hank's party could be heard faintly above the moaning night outside and she wondered what they were doing down there now.

She came away from the window slowly, not making any noise. Roger Gordon was stretched out on the bed, his chest rising with each heavy breath, his eyes closed and his face relaxed. She went over there and stood looking down at him.

"Roger!"

He didn't move and she knew that he was asleep. She found the light switch on the wall and snapped it off. She waited a couple of minutes, watching him there in the deep gray of the room, making sure that he was still sleeping.

Then she took off her clothes and lay down beside him.

She had no way of knowing how long she stayed there like that. She started to get cold and she managed to get the bedspread out from under him and cover herself with that. He groaned a couple of times as she unbuttoned his coat and shirt and she thought that he was going to wake up when she tried to get his coat off. But finally she got his arm free of it and she let it fall on the floor. She took off his other things.

After that she lay there waiting, listening to the wind outside, thinking of nothing except that he was going to be as mad as hell when he woke up.

She wasn't wrong about that.

"Gripes!" he said. "What time is it?"

"I don't know, Roger."

"I must have been sleeping."

"That wasn't all you did," she told him, stretching into the bed. She let one bare arm fall across him and she could feel him grow tense.

"Della?"

"Yes, Roger."

He sat up on the edge of the bed. When he got to his feet she heard him swear.

"Damn!"

He turned on the light and the soft glow filled the room.

He blinked a couple of times, stared at her dress and panties on the floor, then up to where she lay on the bed, the spread barely covering her. His eyes asked her a silent question and she nodded her head, looking away from him coyly.

"I don't know what to say," he said, his hands trembling as he lit a cigarette. "I shouldn't drink that lousy whiskey, but—"

"I hope you didn't tear my dress," she said, making it harder for him. "I just got it yesterday. And—you couldn't wait."

"To hell with the damned dress!"

"That's what you said, Roger. You said for me to take it off, or you'd take it off, or rip it off—you didn't give a damn."

He tried to look at her, but couldn't.

"What else did I say?"

"You said I'd be able to afford plenty of dresses when I'm made manager at Bolton. You said you'd make me a manager."

"Did I?"

"That's what you said. Don't you remember?"

He slowly buttoned his shirt.

"Of course I don't," he said a little angrily, almost to himself. "I remember sitting on the bed, thinking that maybe you'd do all right, and then I got awfully sleepy. That's all."

"I believed you," Della said, talking into the pillow so that it would sound a little bit as if she were crying. "I believed everything you said."

"That's because I meant it."

Her fists squeezed together tight under the bedspread. "About the job?"

"Sure, Della."

She started to relax.

"When?"

"A week from Monday. All right?"

She wanted to laugh and to cry.

"Yes. Oh, yes!"

He went over and stood before the mirror, adjusting his tie. When he had it just right he turned and looked at her.

"About the other things I might have said," he told her. "Let's forget them."

She put her heart in her eyes for him, making it all right for him, smiling up at him as if he were the only man this side of Adam.

"Anything you say, Roger."

He came across to the bed, bent and kissed her briefly on the cheek.

"I'll go back and rejoin the party," he said. "When you get dressed, come on down. I'll tell them that you don't feel so good."

"Yes, Roger."

He went out, closing the door softly behind him. She lay there quiet for a moment and then she started to laugh. It was a funny thing, but she had a lot in common with Roger Gordon.

He was a liar, too.

She'd never felt better in her life.

10

Bolton was a city of considerable size, its center crawling with factories and stores, its scattered residential section spewing out across the city line into Wayne County, where taxes were cheaper. Unlike Port Benson, Bolton had doubled in size the previous twenty years. It was hard to explain what happened to one city and didn't happen to another. Maybe it had been the war. Or a lot of double beds. Or any one of the thousands of things that can happen to the people who live in houses, sleep on their porches in summer, shovel coal into their furnaces in winter, or covet their neighbor's wife at the earliest opportunity.

Della sat at her desk in the office of the Wyandot Roofing Company. At the moment she didn't give a damn about Bolton, the fact that the city was burying its mayor that day, that there was to be a special election and that there was a good chance a Socialist would run off with the trophy. There was just one thing that interested her—business. She'd been in this office for six weeks and business had been good. Business had been so good that her heart hurt just thinking about it.

The door squeaked open and she glanced up from the salesmen's progress chart she had been studying.

"Sorry, Miss Banners."

"That's okay, Margie. Come on in."

Margie came in, and when she entered a room occupied by Della that room suddenly took on a feeling of being overcrowded. Not that Margie was large—she wasn't. She was just big enough in the right places, far developed beyond the high school diploma stage that she belonged in. Margie had dark hair, sweeping back to a cute little bun at the nape of her neck and her black, laughing eyes brought immediate attention to her quiet young face. She was shorter than Della, not quite so full around her breasts, but with round, swaying hips and a middle that was so small that it hardly seemed to exist. Margie was eighteen and every pound of her woman.

"Mr. Bishop called and said he couldn't make it for dinner," Margie said. "He said he'd see you in the morning."

A fine thing! Just when they had a chance to go out for the evening with some respectable people he had to turn up missing.

"Thanks," Della said, pushing the chart aside.

"Oh, that's quite all right," Margie said, going out.

Della stared after her. The little snip had a way of always making you think that she was doing you a favor. That wasn't her only fault. She talked too much and she was too friendly with the customers. She was too friendly with the sales force. And she was much too friendly with Jack.

Della thought a little bit over that promotion business. After that night of the party there had been no question about Roger Gordon's okay of her. He had okayed her as she lay there on his bed, looking up at him. He had stayed over and on Monday he had okayed her in the office. He hadn't lingered long, just signed the necessary papers. It was only then that she learned that Hank got a thousand dollar bonus for making a new manager. She hadn't seen Roger Gordon since, and as far as she was concerned there was absolutely no hurry about it. The next time he showed up he'd probably come looking for what he had been stupid enough to believe he'd gotten from her the first time.

Hank had had a price, too. Della had expected it. Hank was the kind of a guy who'd give you the right time of day—if you'd pay him for the wear and tear on his watch. The day after her promotion, Hank had called her into his office and put a price tag on his efforts. She had expected it might be a night in a tourist cabin or just a wrestling match in the back seat of his Caddy.

She had been wrong.

What Hank wanted of her had been easy enough. He simply requested that she take Jack Bishop along with her as a salesman—Jack Bishop, lock, stock and the quart of Old Harper he'd been nursing since he'd learned of Della's promotion.

She didn't know, even now, why Jack had agreed to the move so readily. He'd cut her short when she'd tried to explain things to him, merely nodded his head, said, "Okay," and gone home and packed his bags. Since that time he had only mentioned his wife once, and that had been on their second day in Bolton.

"Well, Shirley's got what she wants now," Jack had

said.

"And what's that?"

"A check from me every week. And Hank Annabella in her bed every night. Only maybe she'll get fooled about the check."

He'd turned and walked out of the office, slamming the door before she'd had a chance to ask him any further questions.

Della yawned and stretched luxuriously behind the big, polished desk. To hell with Hank Annabella. To hell with Shirley. To hell with—no, not to hell with Jack! Jack wasn't so bad. As a matter of fact Jack could be all right when he wanted to be that way. He was a man and he was an adequate lover and that was more than she could say for Roy and the other jittery, clumsy guys she'd known. She spent a little time wondering about Roy, but not seriously, just in a curious sort of way. She hadn't heard from him since he'd sent her that note shortly after the time he'd been to the apartment. He'd just told her, in a couple of brief lines, that the check hadn't cured her father.

She wondered about her father and mother, and what finance company they were trying to dodge. That put her in mind of money and that she was making plenty of it, and that she hadn't sent them anything for Christmas. She'd put it off, thinking that she'd go up there then, but she'd got her new car just the day before that and she and Jack had gone to an inn in the country and gotten drunker than a couple of skunks eating apple pulp. They'd had fun and she hadn't thought about the annual present again until now.

She took her checkbook from the middle drawer of the desk, wrote a check, making it payable to her mother, in the amount of two hundred and fifty dollars. She tore the check out of the book, blew on it a couple of times, debated about tearing it up when she realized that she was actually parting with the money, then put it in an envelope and addressed it. She sealed the envelope, put a stamp on it—a company stamp—and threw it in the Out box.

She turned her thoughts back to Jack. Why did he always have to screw things up? He never seemed to be where he was supposed to be, when he was supposed to be there. There was this dinner tonight at the country club, with a guy from the bank who could help them with some FHA loans whenever money was tight.

Della picked up the phone. She had to see Jack. Only Jack would know what to say to this banker.

"What number are you trying to call?"

Della didn't know, so she hung up and swore at the operator. She didn't know where to reach Jack. She never knew. Sometimes he'd leave a number at the office, where he could be located, but when she tried to call him she'd been told that he'd never been there and he wasn't expected. Some of the canvassers would make good appointments and turn them over to Jack, but he seldom put in an appearance—unless it was something big. Jack was only interested in the big jobs because those contracts meant big money, no credit problems and fewer calls. And, of course, if Jack got a deal by himself it meant that he didn't have to split the commissions with anybody. Since Della's promotion Jack had not been over-generous in sharing his sales.

She lit a cigarette. This was a hell of a Saturday. Where could Jack have gone?

The phone rang.

"Hello," she said, answering it.

"Yeah. Della?"

"Jack!" She puffed moodily on her cigarette. "Look, mister, when you've got something to tell me, don't call out front. You call me right back here in my office, where I can talk to you."

"That's what I'm doing."

"I meant the first time, a little while ago."

He laughed.

"That was for effect, baby. I was talking with this guy and I told him I had to call my office because I was late already and I wanted to square with the boss. I wanted to put some time-pressure on this guy. And I didn't want any arguments from you while I was doing it."

"You'd better start talking," she said, amused with him now, "or you won't be square with the boss."

"You'll cool down when I give you the news, baby. I just wrote the Bedford Hotel for a nine thousand dollar roof job!"

"You—what! Say that again, Jack!"

"The Bedford Hotel. You know where it is. It's out of town, near Echo Lake, right next to that casino you wrote when you were out with Anderson one day. Nine thousand bucks, baby! Put that on your new business report!"

"I certainly will!" Then, "Oh, Jack!"

She remembered the place. It was a large rambling building painted a sad buff color, with all flat roofs.

"That's why I didn't want to talk to you when I called before. I knew you'd squawk about not going over to the club tonight. Actually, I'll pick you up and we can meet those people out there when you told them we would."

"I don't want to go now," Della said. "I'll put it off until some other time."

Jack swore softly.

Della said, "Now, don't get angry, Jack. I think that dinner with them would be pretty stuffy, and right now there's something else I want to do. I want to talk with you."

"Apartment or office?" he wanted to know. "Or over here at my place?"

"You're home?"

"Sure." He lived in the Langley House, where a lot of old retired people just sat around in the lobby, waiting for nothing.

"Come down here to the office," she said.

"Whatever you say, baby."

She hung up, and as soon as she did she was sorry. Perhaps the apartment would have been more suitable for her purpose. But she guessed that this would be all right. She had an idea that she'd reached a point where she didn't have to go hopping over bedsprings to get what she wanted from Jack or from anybody else.

Della pressed the buzzer on the side of her desk. Presently the door opened and Margie came in.

"Lock up shop," Della told her. "You can go for the day."

"But it's only three-thirty, Miss Banners," Margie said. "I've still got a lot of work to do. And Mr. Bishop hasn't been in for his check yet. I thought I'd better get it ready to mail, or wait and call him when he gets to his—"

"I said you could go! Mr. Bishop will get his check. I'll see to that."

"Oh, I don't like to trouble you with my work, Miss Banners. I don't mind—" the girl's smile wilted under Della's cold stare and she swallowed, hard, a couple of times. "Well, just as you say, Miss Banners. I'll lock up. And thanks."

After she went out, Della wrote a reminder on the calendar to hand Margie her dismissal form on Monday morning. She thought a minute about Anderson and wrote his name down there, too.

Ben Anderson would never make a salesman. His brown eyes were too sad and he felt too sorry for people. Besides, his wife drank a lot and he could never seem to get enough money together at once to buy a decent suit. He went around looking more like a carpenter than a salesman. Then there was that wise-cracking Hendricks who was so smart that he'd lost his car to the loan company. Steve Mulligan, middle-aged and gray, was all right. Steve was steady, didn't give a damn what people said, listened to gripes and forgot them with the speed of a mind that had had years of practice doing it. Danny Starnes was fresh out of the insurance business. He'd been caught adding two and two and getting three for the company and one for himself—and he was making more money than he'd ever made before.

That was her sales force. Not bad and not good. Good with Jack to carry the burden but, she thought, one hell of a poor crew if Jack weren't there.

The canvassers were a sad lot. Old man Lawton had been with the company for ten years, never getting more than one job a week, steadily losing his sight and getting things mixed up all the time. Mrs. Eldridge was a widow with three kids who seemed to be sick about nine-tenths of the time. Arlene Haskell was in her early thirties, hated men, liked women, and was apt to start an argument with her closer in the middle of an interview.

Della laughed and sat there, not turning on the lights, letting the gloom of an early afternoon fill the room. She wondered if she might be on the verge of making her first serious mistake. She decided not to think about it anymore. Some time she would know, but not today—no matter how much she thought about it.

Jack came in around six. He stopped in the doorway and snapped on the lights. He was dressed in a dark gray suit that fit him perfectly.

"Holding a wake?"

"Just trying to see the inside of a dream."

He came over and sat down on the edge of a desk. "What's up, baby?"

"That depends," she said, "on you."

She stood up. It made her nervous for him to sit there above her, looking down. Things weren't that way at all any more. Things had changed. She could fire him this minute and he wouldn't know what hit him. He was so far below her that she had trouble seeing him for distance.

And that was just where she was going to keep him.

She went over and looked at the clock. That wasn't necessary because she already knew what time it was and it didn't make much difference anyway. The curves of her body seeped through her wool skirt and plaid blouse, but she wasn't trying to give him any body charm. He was quite familiar with what she had underneath. She decided, trying to fight the feeling down, that she was just a little nervous.

"Jack," she said suddenly, "do you remember when we came here?"

"Yeah."

"We've been doing fairly good."

"I'd say so."

"But not good enough," she said, facing him.

He shrugged. "Oh, I wouldn't say that. This office was pretty bad to start with. And the town is no lily patch. Wyandot has stuck so many people around here with sloppy jobs that you're lucky if you live to walk to the end of the block. You were smart when you saw that and sold the guys and gals on the idea of working out in the bushes, where there's more money and less resistance."

"I wasn't talking so much about the salesmen or the canvassers, Jack."

"Well, I was. You can only get so much out of them. You can scare the girls, and badger the men, and work with them until you drop dead—but you won't set the world on fire with the bunch you've got. You've got to recruit more, get people who don't know too many of the ropes, people you can train your way. I guess it's none of my affair, but—"

"To hell with them!" Della said.

"What?"

"I said to hell with them."

He got down off the desk and walked slowly over toward her.

"I ought to know you by this time," he said. "But I sure don't. This district was way down when we got here, and you've got a chance to make a real record. I'll help you. But you've got to build up an organization, get new—"

"It isn't the office," she cut in. "Maybe there ought to be something done and maybe I will, but right now I'm satisfied with that part of it as it is. There's nothing wrong with that. What I'm not satisfied about is us."

He stopped a few feet away from her, stood very still.

"Look, baby," he said, "you don't have to take aim when you get ready to throw your hatchet. My back is wide open."

"You can be awfully stupid some times!" Her smile was more of a sneer. "We're not talking about the same thing, Jack. I'm talking about us—money."

She crossed to him quickly. Her hands were doubled up in little fists at her sides and the words seemed to choke and swell in her throat.

"Goddammit, we're not making enough money, Jack!" He grabbed her roughly by the shoulders and the power in his thick fingers stung at her flesh.

"All you think about is money! You're going crazy over money. Why, baby?"

For just a moment she wasn't in that office at all. She was standing, once again, by the house that leaned against the side of a hill that skirted the Willowkill. The wind was blowing and she saw a couple of dry, wooden shingles fly off the roof, sail away into the green alder bushes. Hard drops of rain swept down with the rising wind, raking the countryside. Her mother ran out of the barn, screaming for Della to get over and help put the hay in out of the rain.

She had helped, listening to her father swear and her mother gasp for breath as she tugged at the sodden grass. But none of their work had done any good because the next day they'd had to throw the hay out of the barn, letting it lie steaming in the sun, hoping that it would dry out. But it had rained again that day, and the next, and that winter her father had sold one of the cows because there wouldn't be enough feed and surely not enough money to buy it at the feed store in Harris.

"Money?" Della repeated, sick at the thought of that winter. "Why not? What else would I want?"

"I don't know," he said. "There are other things."

"It's the only thing that makes people different," she said. "You know it and so do I. The people who have the most money are the biggest pillars in the churches."

"I wasn't aware that you had that in mind."

"You needn't be sarcastic. I don't. I'm just telling you. Even in a place like that, the dollar decides whether you have a pew reserved for you, or you stand in the aisle."

"I've never been in a church that crowded."

"Forget it," she said. "I was just telling you how I feel about some things."

"I think I know, Della."

"Then, all right."

His eyes searched her face thoughtfully, seeking something. Then he stuck his hands in his pockets and leaned back, rocking on his heels.

"What's the angle this time, Della?"

"Must there be one?"

"With you—yes."

She took a deep breath and the pack of cigarettes in her left pocket pressed down hard on her breast. She wished that there was a pocket in her skirt. That was a hell of a place for a girl to carry cigarettes; it made her look lopsided. She took the pack out of her pocket and threw it on the desk.

"Well, here it is," she said. "Try to look at this my way, Jack. This is a scramble and you know it. You should. You've been at it so long that you've got your second wind. I don't intend to keep running until that happens to me."

"I had that figured all along, baby."

"How long do you think that this company, big as it is, can last?"

"I haven't any idea."

"Three years? Five years?" She went over and got the pack of cigarettes and lit one. "How much longer than that can it be? Not long. They lie too much to last longer than that. They lie to everybody, about the texture of their shingles, about their guarantees, even about how their jobs are financed."

"I think you're wrong," he said. "People have got short memories. People like to get gypped. People haven't got any sense."

"This outfit is still a bunch of liars!" she said, hotly.

"Oh, I agree." He took one of the cigarettes, held it un-lighted in his mouth and grinned at her. "But, baby, it's just possible that they're going to meet their match."

"It isn't a question of matching them," she said. "It's a question of beating them."

"I wish I knew what you were talking about."

"More money, stupid."

He bent and kissed her lightly on the cheek.

"Tell me the rest of it, baby."

She pushed him away, gently.

"Look, Jack, I've studied this whole thing out since we've been here. I thought I saw it before, when we were working for Hank, but I couldn't be sure. I wasn't in a position to know. It all hinges on the inaccurate way in which most of the jobs are figured by the closers. Even a good closer has to figure his job before he gives his selling interview, or he hasn't got anything real to talk about. Usually he is in a hurry because the client won't let him waste too much time measuring. Right?"

"Absolutely."

"And if he figures the job wrong, quotes the finished

price short, what happens?"

"The loss is taken out of his commission. I've had it happen."

"And you've had years of experience, Jack. But, take the new man—how does Wyandot teach a new man to measure?"

"With a tape—if he can," Jack replied. "Then add thirty percent to that figure."

She nodded, her eyes bright and shining.

"Perhaps you don't know it, Jack, but there is actually a fifteen percent saving on that figure. On the average, the closer's figures are fifteen percent high to begin with—he wants to be on the safe side—and if a new man is not sure of himself it's apt to be even higher. What do you think happens to that average fifteen percent?"

"The customer doesn't get it."

"Silly!"

"Nor the salesman."

"Know any more good ones?"

"I guess the company must keep it."

"Or the manager," Della stated, breathlessly.

Jack frowned, ground out his cigarette in the ash tray and took a couple of fast turns around the office. "So that's it!"

"It's a clover field, Jack."

"Yet I don't see how it could work that way," he told her. "In the first place, the customer pays the company, not you as the manager. I don't see how you could latch onto that surplus—if that's what you're thinking about."

"That's it."

"It sounds pretty difficult."

"I take it that you're not against getting that money; you're just stumped as to how we could go about it."

He sat down on the desk again, remained silent for a long time.

"Something like that," he said finally.

"That's the easiest part of it," she told him.

"You tell me."

"I will. On a job where there is fifteen percent saved, both in labor and materials, we simply save the excess materials and show on my report that they were used. Since we pay the applicators weekly and not by the job, I can charge off the entire labor cost, holding the excess check as to such time as the workers have actually earned it. That's all there is to it."

His glance was sharp.

"Then, why drag me into it?"

"Well, you have a part, too. Your job would be to dig up the shingle and roof jobs where the people would pay in cash—not ask for financing, or a second mortgage, or something like that. Then we use the shingles we swiped, get someone to put them on and pocket the difference. But we have to get our hands on the money before we can cut ourselves in."

He looked at her directly and his face seemed old and tired and worn. She didn't know, of course, what he was thinking about, but she had an idea that it wasn't doing her any good.

"I figured up how much we could have made, if we had been doing that since we got here. It's a lot of money, Jack."

"Yeah?"

"Over four thousand."

Ten thousand dollars, Della thought. Four for Jack.

"If we were still working for Wyandot," Jack said.

"We couldn't get caught."

"Not if we don't do anything."

"Or if we do," she said.

He got up and buttoned his coat. He didn't look at her.

"I don't know," he said. "I guess it would work, but I want some time to think about it, baby. Maybe I'm doing all right as I am, and maybe I'm not. I'll kick the idea around tomorrow and let you know first thing Monday morning."

"What about that Bedford Hotel?" she wanted to know. "Is that a cash job?"

"On the barrel-head."

She got over there to the door before he could open it and walk out. She thought she could see the trace of a smile on his lips, but she couldn't be sure. Her hand found the wall switch and snapped the light out, plunging the office into the deep darkness of the winter's night.

"Jack," she murmured huskily, "why don't you just stay a few minutes more so we can talk it over?"

His hands were already fumbling with her dress. "Sure," he said. "Anything you want, baby."

❚❚

Della closed the door of the office safe and heaved a sigh of relief. She had just successfully passed her first audit. The young man with the wavy blond hair had been there for a couple of days and he had departed that morning, telling her that everything was in good shape. He'd told her that he was on his way to Port Benson and Della had the feeling that the auditor and the salesman with the fingernail polish would have a nice time together.

"What a peculiar man," Miss Carlson said to Della.

Miss Carlson had replaced Margie. Miss Carlson was somewhere near middle age and sort of waspish and at times inclined to be rather silly. Her face held a perpetual look of dismay at everything that happened around her. The main topic of conversation at which she was adept was that of how many cats she had at home, how much they ate and the awful things they did.

"Oh, he was rather nice," Della said.

Surely it had been nice of him not to have discovered

that Della had drained about three thousand dollars from Wyandot in the previous six weeks. On the other hand, there had been no way for him to discover such a transaction. She was damn glad that she had made sure of that. Her charms would have been to no avail with him.

"Mr. Bishop is late this morning," Miss Carlson said looking at the clock. "It's after ten."

Jack Bishop, Della felt sure, represented to Miss Carlson all that was male in the world. Had Miss Carlson been a younger woman, Della would have canned her the second day she was on the job. Since that night in the office—that wonderful night that had lasted until morning—a large part of Della Banners had belonged to Jack.

"Mr. Bishop worked late last night," Della said.

She went across to a desk and sat down and started signing the payroll checks. She wished that she could be sure that Jack had been working late last night. He had told her that he was going to visit the general manager of Henderson and Company, glass manufacturers, with the objective of selling him a flat room job on the complete plant. She had waited at the apartment until after eleven, drinking a little and getting plenty mad, before she'd tried to call him at the factory. No one had answered.

"Hell!" she said viciously, slamming the pen down. "You'll have to do this one over; I signed it wrong."

"Very well."

"I think I'll go in and rest a while." She stood up. "I didn't get much sleep last night."

She hadn't slept at all. She'd waited until two, then tried calling him at the hotel. No, they hadn't seen him. After that she'd gone to bed, but she hadn't been able to sleep. Where the devil could he have been? She'd gone to the phone several times, between three and daylight, but she hadn't picked it up again. She had cursed him roundly. And then she had cried a little bit, the first in a very long time

"You have a sales meeting scheduled for this morning," Miss Carlson reminded her. "They've been waiting for you since before nine."

"I'll hold the meeting tomorrow morning, Miss Carlson."

"Tomorrow is Saturday."

"Don't you think I know that?" Della demanded hotly. "Of course, I know it. When I say I'll have a meeting tomorrow, I mean tomorrow—whether it's Saturday or Sunday, or what the hell day it is."

"Very well, Miss Banners."

"And tell that little Miss Dolan I want to see her in my office, right away."

Della went into her office and closed the door. She was sorry now that she had taken on the four extra canvassers and the seven closers. They had all been cut from the same bolt of cloth. All any of them ever worried about was how big a draw they could get, and was it payday. Keeping them out there banging doors and selling was like pulling spikes out of a white oak plank bare handed. If it hadn't been for her growing bank account she'd have been so tired of the whole mess that she'd have gone out there and fired the lot of them.

She picked up the last quarterly business report. One hundred and seven percent increase over the same period of the previous year. She threw the report into the wastebasket. Where the hell was Jack?

The door opened slowly and Miss Dolan came in. Miss Dolan was about twenty-three, red-headed and blue-eyed. When she had started working for Wyandot as a canvasser she'd had a slim, rounded body; now all that was disappearing into the full lines of approaching motherhood.

"Sit down, Miss Dolan."

Miss Dolan sat, her lips pursed together, her eyes staring down at the floor.

"You know why I sent for you?"

"I—I think so." Miss Dolan's voice was husky and terrified.

"Do you know why I've left you on the payroll this long?"

Miss Dolan's eyes squeezed tight and she shook her head.

"I wanted to see if you'd come to me. You didn't."

The girl said nothing.

"Of course, I should have known better," Della went on. "You're all alike. You just wander around every day, getting bigger, and wondering what it's all about. You're so afraid at a time when you should be very brave."

"Yes," Miss Dolan agreed.

The blue eyes, misty with fear, sought out Della's face. "Who was the man?" Della wanted to know.

Miss Dolan started to cry, her lips drawing together hard and tight and desperate.

"Who was the man, Miss Dolan?"

"I—I don't know!"

The girl's sobs filled the room. She kept shaking her head, saying over and over that she didn't know who the man was, that it was awful, that she wanted to die, that nothing was any good any more.

"It was at that party they had, right after you came," Miss Dolan said, slowly trying to remember how it was. "I went with Danny Starnes. I wasn't working for you then, but he'd talked to me about it."

"The son-of-a-bitch!"

"No, you musn't think that, Miss Banners. I've known Danny a long time and I came right out and asked him, when I knew how it was with me. He says he never touched me. I believe Danny. Danny wouldn't lie to me."

"Well, you didn't get that way watching television, Miss Dolan."

"I got drunk that night," the girl said, all of her shame crowding up into her voice. "I got awful drunk and then

I was in the back of somebody's car. There was three or four of them. I don't know. Honest, I don't know!"

Della's hand shook as she lit a cigarette. She wished that Miss Dolan was anywhere but in her office. She had a strange desire to scream at Miss Dolan, to laugh, to call her names. But she just sat there staring back into those blue eyes, trying to take something from Miss Dolan and finding that there was nothing more to take, to hurt, or to abuse.

"Well, I'm sorry," Della said at last. "Really sorry."

"You are! What about me?" Miss Dolan demanded. "I'm the one who's going to have the kid."

"Why don't you find yourself a doctor?" Della wanted to know. "Get a doctor to fix you up."

Miss Dolan was shocked. Her tears stopped so quickly that it seemed as though she had merely turned off a faucet. "God accepts all children," Miss Dolan said, confidently. Della shrugged her shoulders. "Unfortunately, Miss Dolan, the world is inhabited by people who judge you not by what you may do, but what you get caught doing. Anyway, it was just a thought. I wanted to help you. I really did."

"Thank you, Miss Banners."

"But I can't let you keep on working. You've been canvassing for Joe Williams; he's going good for a new man and I don't want to lose him. Joe's wife has called me a couple of times and said that people who know them are looking sideways at Joe these days. I'll have to get someone else to work with Joe. I wanted you to know, Miss Dolan."

"Yes, Miss Banners."

Della stood up and Miss Dolan got wearily to her feet.

"There's a job here when you get squared away on this thing," Della assured her. "All you have to do is come back and see me."

Miss Dolan nodded, and walked silently to the door. At the door she turned and looked back, her eyes big and frightened.

"Isn't there something that I could do around here, Miss Banners? I'm a good typist, and I know something about keeping books. I wouldn't be out front."

"I said there's a job for you when you get straightened out," Della told her firmly. "That still goes."

"But that's a long time from now, Miss Banners. I haven't got anybody, only an aunt, and she—"

"I told you how to rush things," Della said, going over to the window to look at the African violet plant Jack had given her. "You could be back to work in no time at all."

There was a moment of sharp silence. Then the leaves on the violets jumped as Miss Dolan flung the door open.

"Just remember, Miss Banners, that the same thing could happen to you," Miss Dolan said as she went out.

Della laughed and bent to smell of the violets. She wasn't worrying about anything like that. As long as she was careful—but she couldn't be careful and drink, too. She had acquired a taste for liquor and the way it made her feel, making the world smaller, relaxing her naked body on the bed while Jack became part of her.

Around eleven Jack came in, shouting a good-morning to Miss Carlson that was cut off as he kicked the office door shut.

"Hi, baby!"

"Listen," Della said, "do you remember that party we had just after we got here? The one at that little private club?"

"Sure."

"Well, Miss Dolan got herself knocked up that night."

Jack whistled and sailed his hat across the room; it landed on top of the filing cabinet.

"How nice!"

"Some men got her out in one of the cars," she said. Then, earnestly, "Were you one of them, Jack? Did you go out there to that car with her?"

"Hell, no! My luck isn't that good," he said, with a low laugh.

He went across and hung his coat on the rack. Then he went over to the desk and sat down, got paper and pencil out of the drawer and jotted down some figures. She watched over his shoulder. He subtracted seventy-five hundred from nine thousand and divided the balance by two.

"That mean anything to you, Della?"

She thought back and it came out clear and sudden. "The Bedford Hotel. Seven-fifty for you and seven-fifty for me." Only it hadn't been exactly like that. Her share had been a thousand.

"A headache for both of us."

"Money for both of us," she corrected him.

He threw the pencil down on the desk and stood up straight, facing her.

"Yeah. Money for both of us. That's what you said when you started getting bright ideas when I told you that this was to be a cash job. Just put on four layers, you said, instead of five. Then, you said, we'll split the difference and nobody will know. We split the difference. And they know, baby."

"I haven't the faintest idea what you're talking about, Jack."

"About that damned roof!" he said. "I go home last night to clean up for that appointment I had with the glass company, and the phone rings. It's this guy Snatcher, who owns the Bedford. He's screaming like he's been shot and he wants me to come out there right away. I try to stall him off, but he's jabbering about the cops and law-suits—so I go."

"So that's where you were."

"I got out of there at three this morning."

"You must have rented a room, to stay that long."

"Remember that storm we had the other day?" he demanded, ignoring her remark. "Well, in some places that roof leaked like someone had poked holes in it. I told you, Della, that four layers wouldn't be enough on those sun-decks. Anyway, when I get out there I find this Snatcher snatching out his hair by the handful. He said the company had guaranteed the job and, by godfrey, they'd pay for it. He said he'd sue until he got to his grave. Actually, there wasn't any damage done and by the time he ran out of breath we pretty well decided that all he wanted was to get the leaks fixed."

"I'll send some men up there today," Della said. "Call him and tell him."

"What do you think I was doing out there until three this morning? Hell, there was some stuff we'd left out in the garage, so I went to work, ruined a suit and got the leaks stopped. I had a couple of drinks with the old boy before I left and we parted bosom friends."

"Thanks," Della murmured. A thing like that could be almost as dangerous as looking into an empty gas tank with a match.

"But what happened got me to thinking," Jack said. "Thinking plenty, baby. We'd be in one hell of a spot if some of those jokers ever wrote to the home office, instead of coming through here. I had an idea that Snatcher was just the kind of a guy to do that, whether I got the leaks fixed, or I didn't. So I got to thinking about what I had said to him when I sold the job. Maybe I mentioned Wyandot's name and maybe I didn't. I suppose I did, because it's a habit that you get into. But I do remember telling him about five layers on the roofs, and that we decided not to send him the guarantee because we only put on four and we made up our minds not to stick our necks out on that."

"That was your idea, Jack."

"And a good one, too. I knew what it might lead to.

And it happened—you and your four layers!— just as I felt that it would. So, last night, I tell Snatcher that Wyandot never did do his job, because they didn't have the proper equipment—jacks, and stuff like that. I tell him that his work was done by Shinglers, Incorporated."

"Have you been drinking?" Della demanded. "You must be crazy, Jack. I never heard of such a company."

"You will, baby. That is," he said quietly, "you'll hear about it after we incorporate."

Della shook her blonde head. This just wasn't her day. Things were coming too fast.

"It's really the only sensible way," Jack went on. "We'll be safe, if we do that—no chance for the company checking up on us. If anything goes wrong with one of our deals, it's only us and Wyandot won't know a damned thing about it."

Della's eyes were now closed and the things she was beginning to see were things that would cost Wyandot money. It was a natural. She wondered why she hadn't thought of this herself. It should have been obvious right from the start that this was the way in, which it should be worked. Now Jack had come up with the idea and that spoiled it somewhat, made it more difficult for her to accept.

"Well, I'll think it over," she said.

"We've got to do it, Della."

"We don't have to do anything, Jack."

"No, sure not," he said, disgustedly. "You can even stop breathing. But it doesn't make sense."

She went over and looked at the violets again. She wondered where Jack had bought them. He ought to take them back. They'd never amount to anything.

"I suppose we'll have to do something like that," she admitted reluctantly.

"We could get started on it today."

"Tomorrow," she said. "Tomorrow's time enough."

"Lawyers don't work on Saturday, Della."

"They do—if there's enough money in it. Anybody will."

He came over to her, reached down and snapped at one of the withered purple blossoms with a thick finger. She felt his warm chest pressing against her back and his other hand slid down and around her waist.

"I was going to get you a gardenia plant," he said. "Only they get bugs all over them."

"I like violets."

He turned her around slowly, and his lips came down on her mouth. His hand came up and pressed gently on the hard nipple of one breast.

"I missed you last night, baby," he said. "Let's get the hell out of here."

"Jack you're mussing my hair!"

"I like to do that."

She started to laugh, to seek his arms and the pleasure of him, when the phone jangled, breaking them apart.

"Damn!" Jack said.

"You answer it," Della said. "Tell them I've gone for the day—tell them I won't be back until Monday. Lord, I'm sick of this place! Tell them anything."

Della went over to the supply closet, opened the door and studied herself in the mirror which she had had installed at company expense. She found some bobby pins in a tray and started getting her hair back into place. In the background she could see Jack, his face anxious, listening to some voice on the other end of the phone. He hung up, without saying anything, and just stood there staring at her.

"Something the matter?" she wanted to know, her mouth half full of bobby pins.

"Yeah," Jack said. "That was Western Union. They called to tell you that your father died early this morning."

Della made no reply. She continued to look into the

mirror, putting the bobby pins in place, not missing a stroke.

12

The passing of Chuck Banners was not accomplished without a certain amount of complications. There was no family burial plot—there had been but Della's father had sold the remaining half to someone else years before— and there was no life insurance.

Della visited Mr. Jonah Hoyt, who had charge of the cemetery, and he prevailed upon her to purchase a lot on the extreme side of the cemetery, right near the bank of the Willowkill. She paid for the land with a check. Then she called on the undertakers, a firm of Beldoes and Riggs, Morticians. Both men were rather old and fugitives from their own business—it was simply a question as to who was going to bury whom first. She selected a suit for her father—a shiny one which probably had been worn by one of the partners—picked out a casket, decided that a concrete vault was not necessary, and paid everything in advance.

During the couple of days prior to the funeral Della took a room in the small hotel in town. The bed was hard and there was a community bathroom and it was right over the bar, but it was preferable to her old room on the Banners farm. On the night before the funeral, she drove out to the homestead, finally persuaded her mother to spend the night in the hotel—the fire in the smoking furnace was just about out and there wasn't any more wood to burn, anyway—and together they drove back to town.

The next day at two thirty they went to the undertakers where the services were to be held, only to discover that the funeral had been postponed until the next day. Her mother cried some and did a lot of yelling at the undertakers. Beldoes and Riggs took turns wringing their hands and explaining that the men who had dug the grave had gotten mixed up in their directions and had dug out a hole in the wrong plot.

Very slowly Della and her mother drove back toward the hotel.

"I don't know," her mother kept saying, picking aimlessly at the lint that clung to her black coat. "I can't understand it, but everything your father ever got mixed up into always went tail backwards."

"I guess it did."

"He was always late—behind on everything. He was always late on paying bills, doing the work around the place—and he finishes it off by being late getting buried."

"Well, it wasn't his fault."

"No, I suppose not." Mrs. Banners sighed and pushed the black hat back on her head. She got a finger stuck in the veil and yanked a big hole in it getting loose. "But it's the only thing that ever happened to him that he wasn't to blame for."

It had rained earlier that morning, throwing an icy crust across the macadam, but now the sun was out again. Della drove cautiously, avoiding the puddles of water. The sand that had been tossed around by the township's maintenance crew came up and slapped gently against the fenders of the new Buick.

"He was an awful man," Mrs. Banners said. Della didn't look at her mother because she knew that she was crying and she didn't want to see it. "But I loved him, Della. I did. He was a good man, and smart—but foolish and stupid, too. After we were married I tried to get him straightened out, but I couldn't. I guess I loved him too much to do a good job of it."

Della knew that the years were there with her mother, just as they had been with her since Jack had told her about the telegram. The years of school and snowball fights, the years of hot summers and cold winter drafts through the house at night, the years of wanting and hoping and struggle—the years which, now, meant nothing because time meant nothing. The years which had seemed endless before now passed in a matter of seconds. The touch of her father's beard, the smell of his ungodly pipes, the way he fried his eggs real hard, in the morning—all of these things really gone because people were lazy and there was always too much to remember.

"I'm wondering what you're going to do now," Della said to her mother.

"I was thinking that maybe I'd go up to Olean and visit my sister. I ain't seen Carrie in years."

"I was wondering about the place," Della said. "What happens to that now?"

Mrs. Banners sighed. "Lord, I don't know. It's probably plastered to the roof with mortgages. If I could get some city people interested in it, maybe I could sell. They say that with all this atom bomb talk that people in the city have got a hankering for the hills."

They rode along in silence. Della noticed her, mother looking at the fancy dashboard, the winecolored cushions, the long, sleek hood. They passed the little white house where Mr. Layton had had his law office and where Della had worked. The blinds were closed tight.

"They went to Florida," Della's mother told her, as though answering a question. "Hattie Elms had a letter from Mrs. Layton a while back. She said that she was still honeymooning and that her old man would hardly let her out of bed. He must be an old fool."

Della parked the car in front of the hotel. A humpbacked man in dirty clothes was sprinkling some salt around on the sidewalk.

"I got me a cousin in Port Jervis," Della's mother said, thoughtfully. "You never met Jenny and I ain't seen her in years. They say her husband's got a fine job with the Erie down there. Jenny rides back and forth to New York all the time and it don't cost her a cent. Maybe I'll get down there to see her someday."

Della knew that her mother couldn't make up her mind what she was going to do.

"About the farm, though, I've been thinking on that. I just don't want to go back there anymore, Della. I just stayed there because of your father and because I couldn't go any place else. But now there's nothing there for me and the place is shot to hell, anyhow."

"A change would do you good."

"That's what I'm thinking," her mother said, trying to straighten her hat. "I think if I go up to see Carrie I can get me a job up there in Olean. She does dressmaking and maybe I could help her out. And they got factories there and I can sew faster by hand than some of those chippies can sew with a fancy machine. I could get me a job in one of those factories."

"You don't have to go to work," Della said. "I can take care of you, get the place fixed up for you, and—"

"That don't seem right. Here you've gone and laid out money for this cemetery lot, and the funeral—"

"Well, he was my father, wasn't he?"

"Oh, sure." Mrs. Banners folded and unfolded the veil, finally rolled it into a ball and dropped it onto the floor. She cranked the window up and down a couple of times, watching the motion of the handle. "Sure, he was your father, Della. But that isn't it. The thing I mean is—well, I don't know how to say it."

"You should say it."

"Not now."

"I'd like to know. It won't get any better with age."

"It's hard, Della. I'm not so good at putting things the way they ought to be. It's just—well, you ain't never been like a real daughter to us. I know that's an awful thing to say, Della. Maybe it was his fault, and maybe it was mine.

I don't blame you none, because you're young and you want different things. We never give you a hell of a lot. You always wanted things, more than we could give you, and we never seemed to be able—oh, hell, I've said it. I didn't mean to. And I didn't say it good."

"I'll go along with that," Della agreed, her face flushed.

Mrs. Banners shrugged weary shoulders and rubbed a hand across her face.

"It don't make no difference," she said, "because you been mighty good to us in the last couple of days. And you've been good sendin' us money since you've been gone. This farm don't mean anything to me. Maybe it'll mean something to you some day. Some day when you get married and have kids and like that."

Della shuddered. She could just see herself getting married and fat and pregnant and burying her whole future up there in the Willowkill Valley. She could certainly see something like that. A hundred years off she could see it.

"—just give me five hundred dollars," her mother was saying. "That's enough to get me started up in Olean and pay that lousy doctor off down here. When you hand over the five hundred, I'll sign the farm over to you. Half of it's yours anyway according to law, I guess. But you'd have to take care of the mortgages."

"You can have the money without giving me the farm," Della said. "I don't know whether or not I want the place."

"You don't have to keep it."

Della tapped her teeth with the tips of her fingers. Maybe there was a market for places like that. She could have a new roof and sidewalls put on at cost, and maybe get the porch jacked up so that it would look straight. If she didn't sell it, she could always use it for weekends. Jack had said, once, that he liked fishing, and there were plenty of trout in the Willowkill in summer and good pickerel fishing in the lakes around the county during the winter.

"Well, all right," Della said. "You don't have to do that, but if you want to—why, sure."

"That's the way I'd like to have it. That way I won't have to bother you any more."

Della carefully placed the ignition key in her purse. She looked at her mother sharply.

"I'd like to know just what you meant by that."

Mrs. Banners averted her eyes, following the movement of the people along the street.

"Just this, Della. We—oh, well, you're my daughter and I know that. But—that's all. You have your own life to live and I have mine, what there is left of it. I had enough deals when I lived with your father. I don't want to be near you and have any part of yours."

"My what?"

"Deals."

"I see."

"I—Della, don't think bad of me. I guess I'm just fed up with the way things have been."

"Yes."

"I was pretty sore when you left home, Della."

"Yes, I suppose so."

"I always had an idea that you might hit it off with Roy. He's such a good boy and I'm sure that he loves you. Or he did love you. I guess maybe now he's just sorry for you. Like me, Della. I'm sorry that you think you have to have everything nice in the world in order to be happy. There's more to it than just nice clothes, and money, and a big car like this one."

"Well, for St. Peter's sake!" Della exploded. "How do you like that? I make a success of myself and you feel sorry for me!"

Mrs. Banners' eyes probed at Della in deep concern. Her hands, red and hard from too many washings and too much outdoor work, pressed down into the soft cushions.

"I always did have trouble getting things across." Mrs. Banners sighed and relaxed wearily. "It isn't the car, Della, or anything like that. Not just alone, it isn't that. It's what you've become—the success as you call it."

"Since when has that been such a crying shame?"

"Well, it isn't. Not exactly, with some. But I know you, Della. I'm a woman and I'm your mother and I know. The day you left here you had just one thing besides the car. You know it. And so do I."

Della was silent for a moment, burning inside, hating her mother for thinking things like that.

"And just how do you think I got on?" Della demanded.

Her mother turned her face away and her voice seemed to come from down inside, way deep, where there weren't any tears, or anger, or anything at all except a dry, haunting grief.

"We don't have to talk about it, Della."

"I think we do."

"I'd rather not."

"You started it. Finish it."

"All right. How'd you get this big manager's job you've got?"

"I worked for it."

"And what else?"

"Godammit, I worked for it I told you!"

"Where?" her mother demanded, turning to stare at her. "Where did you work for it? In an office—or in a bed?"

Della felt her face glowing hot, her blood running fast and cold. She could hear her heart thudding rapidly, unevenly, feel the pound of it at the hollow of her throat. But her voice, replying, was steady, cool.

"Thanks, Mother, for calling me a whore."

"Della!"

"That's what you meant, didn't you?" Her voice rose. "Didn't you?"

"No!"

"The hell you didn't!"

"Please, Della. I didn't mean it that way. I'm just all confused. But when I heard about the swell apartment you had, and all, and you started sending those big checks—"

"I guess Roy's been talking to you," Della said, disgustedly.

"He just said how good you were doing, that's all. It was such a short time, Della, and people around started talking about it when they heard. I got so ashamed."

"That damned Roy!" Della said, heatedly. "He's just sore because he hasn't been getting any of it lately!"

"Della! People might be listening."

"It's true."

Mrs. Banners shook her head sadly.

"I wish you wouldn't talk like that, Della. Look at me. Look at me, please. I don't know much—not about business and stuff like that. Maybe I shouldn't have said anything because I only know what I heard on the radio before the tubes burned out and once in a while I look at the papers. I've been up there alone so long, hearing those things that others did, thinking of you, Della, until it almost drove me crazy."

"Well, it was a stinking time to bring it up," Della said acidly. "Dad's up there dead, and all you—"

"Della, you never bothered coming to see him."

"I didn't think he was sick."

"Well, I didn't think he was, either. That's for certain."

Mrs. Banners opened the door and stepped out of the car. Della got out and walked around the long, yellow convertible. Somehow, it seemed to look out of place in the little town of Harris. It was so big that it appeared to be half a block long parked there. Della glanced at the car again and felt good.

They went up the creaking stairs and into the room.

The room was decorated in friendly pink and it had twin beds and two windows with a view of the river valley and the snow-spotted hills in the distance. Mrs. Banners took off her coat and hung it in the closet. Then she struggled out of the black dress—$18.95 in Roberts Clothes down the block, no charge for alterations—and put it carefully over the back of a straight chair by the desk. Then she went over and sat down on the bed. The slip, which was old and pulled up over her knees so that it showed her varicose veins, sagged limply away from her flat breasts. She sat perfectly still, staring at the floor. She didn't even look up when a pigeon hovered near one of the windows, casting a crazy figure on the rug. Once in a while she pushed her upper plate around with her tongue and took a deep breath.

Della sat down in the easy chair, crossed her long sheer nylons and picked up the current issue of the *Willowkill Times*. Although she held the paper in front of her, she didn't read anything in it. She supposed that she ought to call the office and tell them that she'd be a day late getting back. But that wasn't necessary because Jack had said that he'd take care of things while she was gone. Jack, she decided, was a pretty handy guy to have around.

"We can go see a lawyer about the farm in the morning," Mrs. Banners said, moving around on the bed. "We ought to get that taken care of."

"All right."

"That is, if you want to do what I said."

"I'll do it."

The silence in the room sat down between them, holding them apart just as it had been all through the years.

Heavy footsteps sounded in the hall outside, paused before the door of their room. There was a sharp knock.

Mrs. Banners got up and started for the door, stopped suddenly and pressed her hands against her slip.

"You go, Della. I'll wait in the privy."

"Okay.

Her mother went into the bathroom and closed the door. Della took her own time about going over there to see who it was. She had a good idea who it might be.

"Hello, Roy," she said.

She had an urge to tell him that he ought never to wear blue, that he should stick to grays or browns, something warm that would go well with his bronzed face. She didn't. She didn't give a damn if he went around all winter wearing shorts.

"Della, I wanted to call on you and tell you how very sorry I am for what happened. I intended to see you after the funeral, but I understand it's been put off."

"Yes. Until tomorrow."

"That's what I heard." He put one hand high up on the door jamb, leaned against it. "I had an appointment in Hancock for today with a man about a silo. After your dad died I put it off until tomorrow. The man is staying over purposely to see me and I don't see how I can ask him to change it again. So I won't be able to be there tomorrow."

"No."

"I—so I wanted to see you today, to say hello—and goodbye."

"Hello," Della said, smiling; then, more bluntly, without the smile, "Good-bye."

His eyes sought her face and the hardness in them frightened her just a little.

"I wish that you could have seen things differently, Della."

She stood very still, not saying anything, not moving.

"I know I shouldn't be talking to you this way, at a time like this. But I've got to. You've always had the advantage of me, because you've always known how I've felt about you."

"You told me so many times," she reminded him, bitterly.

"A girl doesn't have to be told. She knows."

"Oh, thanks. But a man does. Men are stupid. On that we are agreed."

"Well, I know now how you feel all right."

"You do?" Her smile flashed at him, challenging him, lighting her face.

"You don't feel at all," he said quietly. "You don't feel a thing. Not like other people."

He turned abruptly and walked off down the hall. As he turned at the corner at the top of the stairs, she saw the stern lines of his face crack and break away.

She closed the door, and stood there with her back against it, her body arched. Then she started to laugh. It was so damn funny! And Roy was so wrong, so completely wrong. She felt something all right. She felt that any time she ever wanted him, she could have him. If that ever happened.

But, of course, it never would.

13

After a somewhat precarious birth the firm of Shinglers, Incorporated, began to grow and prosper. An unused barn, which in the days of horses had served as a livery stable, became the home for this young and struggling enterprise. The casual passerby who noticed the small red and white sign above the old sliding door and who desired further information was somewhat surprised to find that there was no office, no entrance and no telephone upon which the owners could be called. This, of course, proved to be detrimental to any loose business floating around, and when Della heard of the situation she immediately talked to Jack about it.

"I think it's stupid to want to shingle that place and

start advertising," he said. "We don't want to compete with Wyandot. That wasn't the idea at all. We just want to steal from them, baby."

It was Saturday afternoon and they were sitting in her office at Wyandot. She had just given Jack a check for seven hundred ninety dollars, which was over and above his pay.

Her own check she had decided to make out later; of course that would be much larger, nearer eleven hundred. There was a bottle on her desk and they'd had a couple of drinks. They were feeling pretty good.

"Please don't call me baby," Della said. "I'm a big girl now."

His eyes raked over every inch of her body, taking off her clothes, putting them back on again. She pulled her legs up under her, feeling the cool leather of the davenport against the silk.

"Everybody in the office thinks I sleep with you," he said bluntly. "Everybody except you and me. And we know better."

"You can say that again," she said.

It had been like that with them, ever since that night when she'd persuaded him to go in with her on this swindle of Wyandot. She kept giving herself reasons for it. She told herself that she was afraid, that she didn't want to get pregnant like Miss Dolan, that all she wanted was to make money and use Jack as a tool for making more. But they weren't very good reasons; they weren't true. Yes, she was afraid, but not of any of those things. Afraid of herself. Afraid of the feeling that she didn't care, that she just wanted Jack, that none of the other things really mattered.

"Some times I can't figure you," he said, pouring another drink. "You can be so warm—and you can be so cold."

"This business gives me the chills," she said.

"When you think of getting caught?"

"Not that."

"Well, what, then?"

"Hell, I don't know!" she said. "Some times you want a lot of things and then they start coming at you so quick you don't know what to do. You don't know what you want. Take money, for instance. You want a lot of it, and you get it; then you want more, but you don't know why you do."

"That hasn't got anything to do with us, Della."

"Well, it has."

That was final, too, she thought. People and love. There was only one way to keep it from ending—cut it off when there was still something left, something that remained to be fulfilled. That way it would never end, never tarnish, always be there with you when everything else had vanished.

Jack looked at her over the rim of his glass and grinned.

"We could make all this work a hell of a lot more interesting," he said.

"Skip it, please."

Those nights and the moments came back, the times he had asked her if she were afraid and she had told him that she was not afraid. And she had not been, then— only later, when it was all over and things started to be the same again.

"Okay, kid."

"Thanks, Jack." She looked down at the floor, not at him. She couldn't look at him because she had to say this and she didn't mean a word of it. "Those nights were a mistake, Jack. We've got to get that straight. We're just in business. We're making money and that's what both of us want. As long as we keep it that way, nothing can happen."

And she couldn't get hurt, she thought. Damn him, some times she wished that she had never met him. So what if he did get her started in this business; what if she'd never have gotten this far without him? What of all that? One little mistake and she could be worse off than she was before. For a few minutes of pleasure she could look like Miss Dolan. Maybe she'd know who the man was—she'd never be dumb enough not to know that—but she'd have the baby just the same. Damn it, what was Jack hanging around for?

"You're keeping the records straight, aren't you?" he wanted to know, taking another drink.

She wished that he'd let that bottle alone. First thing that she knew he'd be on another bender. Well, hell, this was Saturday, wasn't it?

"How about making me one of those, Jack?" She fluffed her hair with her hands, stretched lazily and walked over to look at the violets. She was sorry that she'd forgotten to water them, but now they were dead and it was too late. "Sure, I'm keeping the records straight. You go over them, too, don't you? How can both of us be wrong?"

It was a tough job keeping three sets of books and always having a second person checking on two of them.

He smiled and carried the drink over to her. It wasn't very cold—the gingerale had come from the soda fountain down the street—but it tasted good and it burned just enough as it went down. He went back and set his glass on the desk and pushed his hands deep into his pants pockets.

"Things are good," he announced.

"I wish I could save more money," she said. "I keep spending it like crazy. First it was my mother—I told you about that, didn't I?—and then that new Lincoln."

"I don't know why you bought that."

"Do you think I do?"

"You said you got a good trade-in."

"Well, I did."

"I guess that was it." He bounced the glass in his right hand, and some of the drink slopped over and landed on the floor. "You didn't buy the new car—you bought the trade-in on the old one."

"Maybe that had something to do with it."

"You're always pricing things," he said. "No matter what it is."

"And why not?" she demanded. "The price on anything, no matter what it is, is never right. It's either too high or too low, depending on what you're getting. You have to make up your own mind if a thing you want is worth the price you've got to give."

He sat down on the desk, one leg hanging over the side, looking straight at Della and she stared right back at him. She had the feeling that at this moment they were pricing each other, weighing comparative values, making a final selection. They were both shopping and they both knew it. And it was obvious that they both had a yen for what they saw.

The door of the office had opened so quietly that Della was not aware of the woman until she saw Jack's startled glance. The woman just stood there, slightly inside the door, her dark haired head very high and very proud, her young, supple body erect and smooth in the red sun dress which was only partly concealed by the gray coat which she had flung, cloak-fashion, across her shoulders.

"Hello, Shirley," Jack said.

The girl didn't say anything. Very slowly, very deliberately she came walking across the room toward Jack. His leg, which had been swinging back and forth, stopped dead still. The girl came right up to him, hesitated a moment, and then slapped him full in the face.

"Hello," she said. Then, in the same level, tone, she added, "You bastard."

Jack cocked his head, one cheek reddening, toward Della. He managed a slight grin.

"I don't know if you've had the pleasure of meeting my wife, Shirley. Shirley, meet Miss Della Banners."

"I met her once," Della said.

Shirley laughed.

"So it's Miss, is it?"

"She's the boss," Jack said.

"I'm glad to see you again," Della said. She wasn't, of course, but it seemed to be the right thing to say.

"I'll bet you are."

"You needn't be so nasty about it," Jack said. His foot started swinging back and forth again. He looked at his wife and rubbed his cheek. "What's up, Shirley?"

"I wanted to get in touch with you, Jack."

"You could have called on the phone."

"So you could hang up on me?"

His grin got wider.

"Why didn't you answer my letters?" Shirley demanded harshly. "I wrote you four times and you never answered. Don't tell me that you didn't get them."

"I got them."

"Well, why didn't you write?"

"I didn't have anything to say."

"I don't suppose you had any money to send?"

"Sure, I had money."

"Maybe you think I've been living off the fat of the land," she said bitterly. "Just because you ran off up here, don't go getting any ideas that you don't have to support me."

"I hadn't thought much about it."

"You mean, you don't give a damn what happens to me. Is that it?"

He slid down off the desk and stood up straight, towering above her. Della saw that there was no anger in his face, no visible emotion, nothing at all except a great tiredness.

"I wasn't worrying about it," he said. "I was pretty sure that Hank would take care of you. In more ways than one."

"Jack!"

"Well, damn it, he's been sleeping in my bed—why shouldn't he pay the bills?"

Shirley's lower lip began to tremble.

"That's an awful thing to say to your wife."

"Maybe you two are doing it like you used to," he sneered at her. "Of course it's colder now, but you could both put on your coats when you go out to that shingle pile. Once you got hold of each other back there—"

The sound of her hand against his face cracked in the room.

"You're doing pretty good," he said. "You haven't missed yet."

"You son-of-a-bitch!" she flung at him, the words choking in her throat. "You dirty son-of-a-bitch!"

"Sorry you couldn't stay longer," Della said, trembling with the strange anger that seized her. "It was so nice meeting you again."

"I'll go when I'm good, and ready."

"You're ready."

"Like hell I am! Besides, I don't know why you're butting into this, Miss Banners."

"This happens to be my office," Della said.

"That isn't it." Shirley's dark eyes cleared of tears, flashing dull and hurt as they watched the fall of Della's breasts. "You just think that you mean something to him, that's all. Why? Because I know Jack and he loves women and you're pretty. But that isn't enough, Miss Banners. The only thing that you mean to him is just the same as any other woman would mean. Just a sexy bundle that adds up to a good piece any time he happens to get in the mood."

Della had an urge to pick up the inkwell off the desk and slam it over the top of that dark, arrogant head. She could feel just how it would be, raking her fingernails across that alabaster face, seeing the blood run, hearing this bitch scream. It had never been that way with them; it never would be like that—because she, Della, would not permit it.

"Mr. Bishop is an excellent salesman," Della said levelly. "As his wife you may not have recognized that. As his boss, I have. But that wouldn't seem to be much of an excuse for you to slander me."

The hard veneer that Shirley Bishop had put on her face chipped and cracked and fell away like old plaster tumbling off a wall.

"I'm—I'm sorry," she said, looking around the office as though seeking a means of escape. "Honestly sorry."

"You should be," Jack said.

His wife's eyes sought and found his face.

"Perhaps we should get a divorce," she said.

Jack shrugged.

"I wouldn't have to go anyplace else. They can be fixed up, right here in New York State."

"I hadn't thought much about it, Shirley."

"Well, I have."

"Then I'll start thinking about it."

She pulled the coat closer around her shoulders, hugging down into it like a child wandering around in a storm.

"I want a divorce, Jack," she said. "I've thought about it and I want one. You're married and you lead your own life. What's right about that? But when a woman does it, or it looks like she's doing it, or she has a man visitor to her house, the neighbors say she's running a cat house and her husband says she's a tart. I'm sick of hearing those things, of having people think those things. I won't stand for it any more." Her voice rose shrilly. "Do you hear me, Jack? I won't stand for it. I've had enough!"

He reached out his hands and held her away from him, saying nothing, the color of his face a grayish white except where she had struck him.

"Why do you want a divorce, Shirley?"

"I told you."

"You didn't tell me."

"It's none of your business."

"But it is."

"Well, ask yourself. You should know."

"All right," he said quietly, giving her a little shove away from him. "You can have your damned divorce!"

For a brief moment they remained motionless, he with his hand on her arm—lightly, almost gently now—and she with her head held high and proud, fighting back the tears, managing a weak smile, struggling to find the words that would cut the past away from them clean and straight.

"Thanks, Jack," she murmured.

He turned from her and walked to the door, opened it.

"You're welcome," he said.

Shirley Bishop walked out slowly past her husband, only her tears saying good-bye to them. He closed the door after her and walked through the strong scent of the lilac perfume to the desk. He picked up his drink and put it away in a hurry. He poured another drink, pausing a couple of times to glance at the closed door.

It was so quiet in the office that Della could hear the hum of the electric clock on the desk. Outside, a car back-fired, sputtered and died and stillness came to the room again. Jack started to pour another drink, hesitated, then took a long belt from the bottle. He made a wry face and grinned at Della, but she had the uncomfortable feeling that he did not see her. He was looking at the door, and she knew that he was seeing his wife, her dark hair, her dark eyes, trying to straighten out in his own mind just what had happened.

Della went over to the davenport slowly, her hips sway-ing, her body swelling out big and alive almost to the point of ripping the seams of her skirt. She sat down, with her legs out in front, long and straight and smooth. She leaned back against the soft cushions and stretched, her arms behind her head. The filmy material of the blouse pressed tight across her breasts and the nipples formed soft dark circles through the net of her sheer brassiere. Her lips were parted and moist and her throat felt dry and hot.

"Della! Beautiful Della!"

She had wanted him to say that. She had known that he would say it. She was beautiful and she knew it, and she had called upon charms to help her before. But this time it was different. This time it was real and for keeps. This time she wanted Jack more than she had ever wanted any man, more than she had ever desired anything else before. She wanted him more in this minute than any woman had any right to want any man. This was, she thought, the end of wanting because beyond this there could be no more. This was all that there was.

"Della," he said, "it's getting late."

"I know it."

"We could lock up the office now and go."

"There's plenty of time."

"I guess you don't want to go."

Through her half-closed eyes she saw his face coming nearer, heard his shoes shuffling against the tough bristles of the carpet. In another moment she could no longer smell the lilac perfume, only the cigarette smoke on his breath and the faint trace of shaving lotion that still clung to him.

"I said I guess you don't want to go."

She did not reply, but her lips were smiling up at him, telling him everything that he might want to know. The davenport groaned slightly, protesting against the weight of his body.

"Della!"

His hands, big and clumsy and harsh, fumbled with the buttons on her blouse. She felt the coolness of his hands against the growing hardness of her breasts, felt the rising tide of passion become bigger, almost intolerable within her. He swung his body around, pressing down on her, lifting her legs to the davenport, forcing her back into the deep corners of the cushions.

Her own hands raised and touched his hair, his cheeks, his lips. With a sudden little cry her arms encircled his neck, drawing him to her, crushing their bodies together until they seemed to be one.

"Darling!" she moaned, fighting for her breath, grasping for every precious moment that belonged to them now. "Jack—Jack darling—we should lock the door."

"Aw, baby, to hell with the door!"

"Please!"

"I said to hell with the door!"

"Yes," she murmured as his hands found her and the moment closed in on them. "Yes, darling, to hell with the door!"

The door didn't get locked that night.

14

A few weeks later Shirley Bishop left for Reno and a quick, uncomplicated divorce from Jack, Miss Dolan gave birth to a squalling baby girl and the spinster who had taken Margie's place in the office got severely bitten in the leg by one of her cats.

It was Monday and the week was just starting and Della sat in the office, deep in a sour mood. All the night before she had been at her desk, struggling to balance the books. Jack had stopped by around midnight and they had killed a fifth of Johnny Walker, talked until after three. After he left, she sat there alone, the liquor muddling the figures, as she unsuccessfully tried to make sense out of her troubles.

The phone rang and she picked it up.

"Wyandot Roofing Company." She tried to sound cheerful.

"Hello, baby!"

"Jack! I want you to get right down here. When I called at eight you said you'd come right up."

"Went back to sleep."

"Well, now that you're awake, how about getting down here?"

"Breakfast first."

"Breakfast later," she told him. "That fairy will be here to go over the accounts some time today. You were going to help me last night—remember?—but it didn't work out that way."

"Why don't you stop worrying?"

"I told you why."

"Okay. I'll be down."

He hung up and she sat there smiling at the phone. Jack was all right. He was pulling in a lot of business. Now that Miss Carlson was occupied at home, soaking her sore leg and trying to settle the cat revolution, Della had all the officework to do. Jack had been riding herd on the sales staff and taking care of everything that pertained to Shinglers, Incorporated. That last wasn't so good, because with Jack in the financial picture of things it was necessary to cut the cake fifty-fifty whenever it was divided. Yet for the first time in her life she had a man she wanted so badly she could never get quite enough of him, even though they slept together every night.

A half hour later Jack came in. There were large, dark circles under his eyes.

"Good morning, boss," he said.

"Good morning, Jack."

They always greeted each other this way, even though they had just crawled out of the same bed only a few minutes before. So far as they knew, none of the help had associated them with Shinglers, Incorporated, definitely classified their tooth brushes as frequently sharing the same rack, or suspected them of any acts of disloyalty toward Wyandot.

"Where the hell is everybody?" Jack wanted to know.

"This is Monday."

"Yeah, that's right. And no one reports into the office on Monday."

"No. Miss Carlson is still in bed with her cat bite." Della thought about that a moment, then laughed. "Or a man."

"I can't picture Miss Carlson as being immoral enough to go to bed—even alone," Jack said. He started to take off his gray topcoat, but changed his mind and left it on. "Listen, baby, I've got a lot of things to do today. What say we get down to business so I can blow out of here?"

"Well, look at the ball of fire!"

"Those fellows we've got working for Shinglers haven't had any jobs since the middle of last week. They called me Saturday night about it. They said that if they didn't get more work they were going to put in for a job with Wyandot."

Della's face grew serious. "I don't want them hanging around here, Jack."

"They won't, baby. I'll snow them under with work. I'm going to take a ride up near the Willowkill today. We haven't worked that part of the country as we should have. Some of those farmers up there use their corncribs to keep their money in. I'll pick up some jobs."

Della had meant to have the old farmhouse done in white asbestos, use it as sort of an advertising medium. But she hadn't gotten around to it and maybe it was just as well, because she had an idea that some people in the Willowkill Valley didn't think very highly of her, or of what she might do.

"Okay," she said. "Let's get to work."

They went out into the front office and she got the huge

ledger out of the safe. Down at the bottom of one of the pages she had made a notation which read, "$3,000?" penciled in lightly so that it could be easily erased.

Della sat down at Miss Carlson's desk, found a pencil and chewed thoughtfully on the end of it.

Jack whistled. "Three thousand!"

"It isn't much," Della protested. "You figure the other thousands we've got, against it, and it isn't much."

"That depends on whether it's an overage or a shortage."

"It's a shortage, Jack."

"Then it's a lot."

He pulled up a chair and she started calling figures off to him. He wrote these down in various columns, separating the straight roofs from the flat-roof jobs, segregating the flappers—these were the loose shingles that buckled in the wind—from the hard asbestos that got the long rust stains on them from the nail heads. At the end of a half hour they had been through all the accounts. Della put the ledger away, sighed hopefully and went to work on the adding machine. Later she checked the tape against what he had written down and went over and glanced at the ledger.

"Well, baby?"

The words stalled in her throat. She told herself that she had to think, but her mind was numb from too much thinking and she couldn't do any more of it. She told herself that this was impossible, but it was possible because it was right there with her. She could add it backwards and it would still come out the same.

"Jack," she managed finally, "we'll have to put that money in. We'll just have to."

"That's a lot of money, baby."

Her eyes flashed, and her voice was low and tight. "Don't you think I know it's a lot? I know just as much about that as you do. And stop calling me baby!"

"Well—"

"We're going to deposit that money now, Jack! We simply have to. It's lucky I knew the auditor was coming, and I wouldn't have known about that only the home office tried to make a reservation at the hotel for him on Friday and the hotel wouldn't accept it. Filled up, they said. So the office called here to get me to fix things up." She laughed nervously. "I'll fix things up all right! Why, if he had walked in here and found things like this it would have been—ghastly!"

"You're not kidding."

She went over and put the ledger back in the safe. "How come the old lady didn't find it out? She closes out the books, doesn't she?"

"Why, no. I do that myself."

"I didn't know you did it every month."

"This is a business, stupid."

"Then it must be your mistake, Della."

Very deliberately he lighted a cigarette, blowing the smoke in little rings around them. She felt the tenseness rising within her, felt the question forming itself into words, felt the fear that only the terror-stricken can feel.

"We don't have that much money, do we?" she asked, afraid of asking it.

She was surprised to realize that she did not know. At the beginning she had known everything so completely that she had taken it to bed with her every night. But since Miss Carlson's accident she had lost track of the whole picture, she saw only a small part of it, just the part where the money came from and nothing of where it went to.

"Oh, we've got that much," he assured her. "But it hurts to part with it. I know that we've made a lot, but we've also spent a lot. You've blown a lot of money on clothes, Della. You don't need clothes to make yourself look beautiful. You didn't need that stone marten. You sure as hell didn't need that."

"I wish I hadn't bought it," she admitted. "It smells like an old horse when it gets wet."

"And I don't understand how you were such a soft touch for that Miss Dolan to get five hundred off you."

"I don't know either," Della said.

But she knew all right. That day Miss Dolan had come up to the office—just a week before her kid was born—she had looked pretty bad. She'd been wearing a coat that she couldn't button and after she'd taken it off Della had felt sick when she saw how the dress hiked up over the huge shape of the baby inside of her, lifting the hem so that her knees were exposed. Miss Dolan had done a lot of crying, yelling that she'd probably wind up having the kid in somebody's alley and dropping it on a stranger's porch. She said that the local hospital wouldn't let her come in unless she had the money to pay them. She'd been to a finance company and tried to borrow the money but she didn't have a job, or anything, and the man there couldn't let her have anything unless she could show some kind of security. She said her teeth needed fixing, after the strain the kid had put on her, and she wasn't sure how long she'd be able to keep her room and that she hoped she'd die.

Della had been honestly moved by the girl's plight, and she had finally taken a note for five hundred dollars and Miss Dolan's promise to pay her back as soon as she could return to work. Miss Dolan had been out of the hospital some time now, and she still hadn't showed up at the office.

"You won't ever see those five bills again," Jack said.

"When she gets back to work, she'll start paying me. I'll take it out of her wages."

"You'll have your hands full doing that."

"I don't know why."

"Because she's working, baby," Jack said. "She's working out of Nick's Bar and Grill, on South Street. She gets twenty bucks a night."

Something cold gripped at Della's heart.

"They say she's doing pretty good," he went on. "They say that the fellows think she's all right."

"I don't want to know about it."

"You should. It's your five hundred."

"I'll forget about it."

"You had her figured all wrong," he said. "They say that she was doing the same thing in high school. Then, last year, she met some guy—a lawyer—and she liked him a lot. She met young Evans one night and went out to that party with him. She got a few drinks and she let them have their way. She knew what she was doing all right. Hell, it was just an occupational hazard with her. But she got fixed up that night and after she left here she tried to put the bee on the lawyer guy. He went for it for a while, paying her some, until he heard about the night of the party. He cut her off, but good. That's why she came to see you. That's why you're stuck on that note. She's back in business again."

He wandered aimlessly around the office. Della tried to think of Miss Dolan being a prostitute. It made her just a little bit weak. That was a hell of a way to make a living.

"We'd better get this money straightened out," he said. "If you need three thousand bucks, I guess you need it. Easy come, go the same way."

She was pleased to hear him talk like this. Now they were working together again, not bickering and tearing Miss Dolan apart, but doing the right thing to assure that nothing would happen to what they had.

"We'll get it back." She went over to where he stood by the window. She leaned up against him, holding him tight in her arms. "We'll get it back so fast, honey, that we'll never miss it."

His lips brushed her cheek.

"I'm getting my money's worth," he said. "Just knowing

you."

It felt so warm, so good, just being there next to him.

"We're both getting our money's worth," she whispered.

He laughed and tickled her in the ribs and she screamed playfully. He gave her a parting slap on the derriere, and went over and picked up his briefcase from the corner by the filing cabinet. Jack always carried a briefcase although there wasn't much in it of any value to him in selling. The closer's kit of sidewall and roofing shingles was very heavy and was generally kept in the car. Della often thought that the briefcase gave Jack a sense of importance.

"I'll give you a ring tonight," he said. "Maybe before that, if I round up a job. Only thing is, you see, for Shinglers we've got to have the cash on the line. That's pretty hard sometimes."

"I've been thinking about that," Della said. "I've got to go to the bank this morning, anyway, to straighten out this mess we're in, so I'll talk to them about it. I think we can make some kind of a deal to have the work financed through FHA."

"You should have done that before, when you were talking about doing it."

"I know it. It was just one of those things."

"Well, it's still a good idea." He opened the front door. "Luck to you, baby."

He went out and she glanced at the clock. It was almost ten. She had to get to the bank right away and get that three thousand on deposit. For a moment she was furious with Miss Carlson and her cats, because there wasn't anybody to leave in charge of the office while she was gone. Finally she arrived at a quick decision, put a note on the door that she would be back in five minutes—people would wait because they had no way of knowing when the five minutes started—snapped the lock on the door and went out and slammed it shut.

She backed the car out of the narrow alley, made a U-turn and headed up the street. Four blocks farther on she turned in at a side street and parked in front of a three story brick building. She got out of the car and went quickly up the walk, went in through the front entrance and bounded quickly up the short stairs.

Inside the apartment she went directly to the Old Dutch bookcase, opened up a bottom drawer and took out the checkbook for Shinglers' Incorporated. She glanced quickly through the stubs and noted that the balance Jack had recorded opposite the last entry showed fifty-four hundred dollars. She smiled happily, started to hum, and carried the checkbook over to the small console table. She used the pen from her pocketbook and with a flourish wrote a check payable to cash in the amount of three thousand dollars. After that she put the check in her pocketbook, returned the checkbook to its hiding place and left the apartment.

When she got down to the porch she noticed that the mailman had been along and that there was a letter in her slot. She didn't open the letter until she was once again seated on the comfortable front seat of the Lincoln.

The letter, which was from her mother, was written in a scrawling backhand that came close to defying any kind of English interpretation. However, Della managed to gather that her Aunt Carrie had suffered a light stroke and that her mother was now conducting her sister's dressmaking business. Her mother said that she was well, repeated this a couple of times, and told Della that she had received the township tax bill on the farm which really should have been sent to Della and which she had mislaid. She would send it along as soon as she found it.

Della read part of the letter through again, returned it to the envelope and started to put it in her pocketbook. Then she changed her mind about that, tore the letter into small pieces, put her hand out of the window and let the wind carry the white fragments away in a quick swirl.

Hell, her mother would write again and she could get the address off the next envelope.

Della drove straight to the Merchants Bank. There were a couple of parking places in front of the building, and she managed to get the big car parked in at the curb.

The sad face of the elderly clerk brightened considerably as he noticed Della. He looked her over, seeking her ever-present plunging neckline. She let her coat slide apart, giving him the show, and his smile told her that he'd like to know more about what was down there.

"Good morning, Miss Banners."

"Hello, John."

He took the deposit book for Wyandot, checked her figures on the deposit slip she had prepared, turned her check over a couple of times, nodded his head and made the entry.

"I'd like to see the president of the bank," Della said.

"Mr. Marvin?"

"Well, someone who can tell me about FHA loans."

"Oh. Well, Mr. Marvin is busy right now. But Miss Logan, third window down, handles most of the FHA business. She could give you any information you might want."

"Thank you."

She swayed her hips a little and walked down to the third window. She felt good. That three thousand changing hands had made a lot of difference. As soon as the auditor was gone she'd get it back, come hell or water six feet deep. Maybe she'd never find where she'd made that error, but she'd get it back. Double. Or triple.

Miss Logan proved to be a woman who had a rather high opinion of her own personal importance. Della told her what she wanted and Miss Logan opened a little door that buzzed all the time while it was unlocked and ushered Della to a seat at a metal topped desk. Then Miss Logan sat down opposite, adjusted her large rimmed glasses several times, frowned darkly, shuffled some papers in a drawer, and said:

"Of course, I am very busy, Miss Banners, but if you would state your needs as concisely as possible I'll try to be of help to you."

"I just wanted to find out something about FHA loans. How do you go about applying for them? I mean, I think I have some business I can throw your way and I'd like to know what it's all about."

"This would be a loan for yourself?"

"No. For customers of mine who want to buy roofing."

"Then that would depend on the customer," Miss Logan said. "We can give you a general outline, the standard procedure for making application. However, each case is individual. Much is determined by what we learn from our credit report."

Miss Logan stopped talking, pushed a button on the side of her desk and the door started buzzing again. Miss Logan looked past Della and nodded her head.

"I think John would like to speak with you, Miss Banners," she said.

Della turned her head slightly and glanced at John. John's gray eyes were sad and pained. Della had a feeling that something was wrong.

"Yes, John?"

He wasn't looking down the front of her dress now, although there was a lot there that he hadn't seen before.

"Sorry to bother you, Miss Banners." He coughed a couple of times, politely, as he was supposed to do. "But there seems to be an error in your account. I—I'm glad I caught you before you left the bank."

Della could only nod, dumbly.

"That check on Shinglers, Incorporated, for three thousand dollars can't clear the bank. I just checked—we always do that right away with large amounts—and there's only about eleven hundred in the account. I thought you'd want to know right away."

The noise of the bank came around her, the sounds of people talking and laughing, the rattle of money on the hard counters. But for that brief moment Della Banners sat there entirely alone, not seeing or hearing much of anything.

"Thanks," she mumbled at last, holding her voice steady. "Thanks so much, John."

15

That night Della waited at the apartment for Jack Bishop, impatient and angry. It had been one hell of a day. The money shortage had been bad enough, but that situation had only been temporary. The bank had, in the end, loaned her an additional nineteen hundred dollars on her car and and the fur coat, and now she was in hock up to her neck again. She was disgusted, and as she sat there near the phone, she showed every bit of it.

Her face twisted as she thought about Jack. He had fixed things up so that she didn't know where she stood. She had been over the checkbook for Shinglers, Incorporated, and that had balanced, from what she could see, but the bank hadn't seen it and that was what counted. She wished that she had gotten a statement from the bank, but she hadn't because she'd been so upset and scared that she'd forgotten about it. She wished that she had never met Jack. She wished that the roofing business was something that she'd never heard about. She wished to heaven that Jack would call.

About seven the phone rang, but it was just a lineman testing the wires. Della swore at him and hung up. She got up and went out to the kitchen. She got a bottle down from a shelf, washed out a glass in the sink, managed to pry a couple of ice cubes loose from the tray in the gas refrigerator, and poured herself a jolt of Johnny Walker. The liquor burned in her throat and the warm glow, deadening some of her ache, spread through her body.

A few minutes later she decided it was hot in the apartment, so she kicked off her shoes and went into the bedroom and took off her suit. She walked to the mirror and stood there looking at herself. She wore only a garter belt, brief panties and a net brassiere. The soft white of her flesh gleamed through the net that cupped gently at her breasts. Rapidly she unhooked the brassiere and slipped it off.

She turned her side to the mirror and now she was disappointed. Her flat little belly had just the trace of a bulge. She knew that she had been drinking too much, but she'd given up the beer and liquor wasn't supposed to be fattening. She couldn't cut down much on food because she never ate much, anyway. Probably she'd have to make up her mind to start wearing a girdle. She hated the thought of that but maybe she could get a lightweight one that would hold her together four ways at one time.

The robe which she put on was long and black and it flaunted every curve of her body. She was just tying the bow when she heard the apartment door open and close.

She came out of the bedroom just as Jack picked up a cigarette out of the small ivory box on top of the radio. He looked at her, grinned and whistled, and turned the radio on. His eyes followed her as she walked slowly across the room, the sheer material of the robe hissing with every step. The music on the radio came in soft and low and she kept right on walking.

"Hello, you bastard," she said.

He looked at her closely, his eyes narrowing. He held the unlighted cigarette in his hand.

"You've got one hell of a nerve, Jack, coming here."

He said nothing. He put his cigarette in his mouth and lit it. The smoke came out of his nostrils in a rush. Her right hand swung in a wide arch, and her fingers numbed with the force of the blow against his cheek.

"What was that for?" he wanted to know.

Her lips curled.

"We share everything fifty-fifty, don't we?"

"Sure."

"Well, damn it, I got slapped in the puss today and I'm just passing your share along to you."

He rubbed the side of his face.

"Nice of you to have remembered me."

"And so nice of you to have told me that that check for three thousand wouldn't be any good," she said, bitterly. Then, remembering all of it, "You're a stinker, Jack!"

"The money should have been there," he said. "I thought it was there."

"From over five thousand to less than two in one short hop," she sneered, turning away. "You put me in a nice hole, a big hole, a hole almost without any bottom."

"I'm sorry as hell, Della."

"You're sorry!" Her laugh was short and sharp. "Did you ever try to square a set of books by being sorry? Did you ever keep one jump ahead of an auditor because somebody else was sorry? You're damned right you didn't. And neither did I."

The radio started to pound out a tune of boogie-woogie. The table lamps threw little streaks of soft light around the room. She turned and saw him sitting over on the davenport, his chin in his hands, his eyes watching the carpet. She went over and turned the radio off.

"You took that money, Jack." She wasn't asking a question; she was stating a plain fact. "You took it and never told me."

"Look, Della, I—"

"You took it!" she shouted at him. "Why? Why?" He stood up and pushed his shoulders back square. "Yeah, I took it," he said, his voice thick. "I took it, but—"

"Why?"

"For Pete's sake, will you stop screaming?" he demanded, his face getting dark. "I needed the money. Why else would I take it?"

"I don't know," she admitted weakly.

She went out into the kitchen and poured another drink. The ice had melted to water in the glass. She poured some ginger-ale in and it foamed up and spilled over the top. She took a long drink and walked back to the living room, carrying the glass.

"I want to tell you what happened," she said. "I want to tell you what happened, so that you know, so that there's no misunderstanding."

"Okay. I'm listening."

"I went to the bank this morning and made a deposit. I made an ass out of myself."

"You said that before."

"I'm telling you all this," she said harshly. She sat down on the arm of one of the big easy chairs. The robe parted in the middle but she didn't bother to close it. "You just do the listening, Jackson."

"Yeah, I'm doing that."

"After that I went back to the office," she said. "But not right away. Not until I had crawled around and put the car and everything else on the block to raise the money. But when I did get back to the office I find the auditor out in front, sitting in his car and making eyes at the queer who works in the store down the street. I got in the office first, without him seeing me, and rubbed out those pencil marks in the books and made the entry for the day. Pretty soon he came in and I shut him in my office and let him knock himself out with the figures."

"What happened?"

Della felt the cold feeling she had experienced that afternoon coming over her again. It started somewhere near the pit of her stomach and flowed through every part of her.

"The roof fell in," she said, growing tense. "He questioned the large deposit this morning. He wondered what the reason for it was, since our recent volume of cash business—because of Shinglers—hadn't been very large."

"You could have told him something," Jack said, sitting down again. "I never knew of a time when you couldn't think of a fast one."

"Do you think I didn't talk?" She swallowed the rest of the drink hurriedly. "I told him that the office girl had been sick and that things hadn't gone too good. I told him that a lot of people came in and made their monthly payments in cash. That was a dilly, because he wanted to see the records on that. I told him that I hadn't had time to post them, that I had the slips some place but I couldn't remember where I'd put them. So he stopped talking about that and went back at the books some more. Then he found this other thing. It was the other thing that really upset him. You know what I'm talking about, Jack."

She paused for a moment so that the force of what she was saying would reach him with all the strength she intended to get into it. And she saw that it was reaching him, making him cringe there before her, stripping him of everything she had ever seen in him. She felt dirty, as if she needed a bath, as if she wanted to be sick right there and then.

"Go on, baby." His voice was barely a whisper and he wouldn't look at her.

"Don't worry about that, Jack. You're getting all of it. You know it all now, but I'm telling you the story again—my way."

The room wasn't very large and they were in it together—but they had drifted miles apart. Perhaps, Della thought, it had been like this right along. Maybe there never had been anything.

"That fairy auditor goes to the bank and gets the

checks," she said. Even now, remembering, her voice sounded far away, as if she weren't talking but listening while all this happened to someone else. "He came back and sat there at my desk for a long time, studying the checkbook, matching it with the checks that I had written during the month. They all fit—except one. Then he starts checking the blank checks in the book, trying to figure out where this check for three thousand dollars, made out to cash, came from. He found it all right. It had been torn out a couple of pages from the back. Just the way you tore it out, Jack."

He still sat there, bent forward as though in pain, staring at the carpet, not saying anything. She wanted him to talk, to shout, to do something. Even if he got up and came over and struck her, that might help. Just having him sit there and accept all that she said so calmly was what tore at her insides.

"Jack." She wished that she had another drink, but it seemed like a long way to the kitchen. "I never wrote that check. It looks like my handwriting, but it isn't. You wrote that check, Jack. You signed my name to it. You're the only one who could have done it. It was you, Jack. You! Damn it, why did it have to be you!"

He got up then, slowly. He stood up tall, facing her, and his eyes were clear and steady.

"I told you I needed the money, Della. I guess I didn't think—didn't realize what I was doing. I was under such a strain, such a pressure, that I couldn't think straight."

"Just try to put all that in the bank," she said, laughing at him. "They wouldn't let you in the door."

"All you ever think about is money," he said. "You're going nuts over money, baby."

"Three thousand dollars worth," she reminded him.

"I went to the office one night and you weren't there," he said. "You weren't at the apartment, either. I didn't know where you were. I went back to the office and waited for you, but you didn't show."

"So you just sat down and wrote a check for three thousand—just to get even because you couldn't find me."

His gaze was direct.

"I don't care for your humor," he said. His grin was broken and crooked. "Well, I waited for you that night. I wanted to talk to you. I kept walking around the office, looking, trying to think. I must have tried to call your apartment a dozen times. You'd left Wyandot's checkbook on your desk and I sat down and looked at it. I tried to think, but nothing happened. So I wrote the check, just as you said. I cashed it at the bank the next day. It—by that time it was too late to talk to you."

"It's somewhat later now," Della pointed out, drily.

"After that," he went on, "I needed a little more money. I was afraid to write another check, but this time I thought of the Shinglers' account. I wondered why I hadn't thought about it before, but I hadn't. I went down to the bank and dug into that. I planned—honest, Della, I planned to make everything right by the end of the month."

"Well—can you?"

"You clipped me," he said, ignoring her. "You clipped me all the way through. I don't know for how much, but I know that you did it. We never split even—only what you wanted to split. I never kept track of anything. What the hell, I never figured that I'd want the money. I had enough—until this came up. Then—"

"Can you straighten it out in two weeks? By the end of the month?"

"Now, Della—"

"You said you were going to. Can you?"

His reply whipped at her across the room.

"I don't know!"

An almost blind fury seized her, a fury that saw their nights and their days and their plans together fall apart and drift away.

"You'll pay it!" Her breasts rose and fell sharply and her eyes stung with the tears. "You'll pay every cent of it, Jack. You can count on that."

"Maybe I've got more coming than I took, baby. You've got to figure it that way, too. I never did before, but I'm doing it now. We had a business and half of it belongs to me. I never got half. You know that, baby."

"Stop calling me baby!"

"Della. You know that, don't you?"

Her chin rose stubbornly and she knew that she had him now, that there wasn't anything at all that he could do about it.

"I'll get every bit of that money," she said, slowly. "If it takes me from here to the grave to do it."

His long calculated look, the slight smile that pulled down the corners of his mouth, told her that it would take almost that length of time to do it.

"You are a bitch!" he said.

Her laugh was something out of their past together.

"You steal from me and that makes me a bitch!"

He shrugged.

"It's true, baby. But not because I stole the money, as you put it—or borrowed it, as I think of it. It's because—you've not once asked me why I took it. I told you that I had been desperate, but did that make any difference to you? No. You don't care about any trouble I might have had. Just the money—that's all you care about."

"But I am interested in you."

She came across the room toward him. Her head was high and proud and golden. The shadows of the room seemed to radiate from the brightness of her, the half-smile on her lips. He was so good looking, she thought. A little dark maybe, but strong and powerful, with big arms that could hold her safe and warm. He was her man and he had done a lot of wrong. It made a difference, of course, but that's the way it was and it was only a small part of the whole pattern that belonged to them.

"All right, darling," she said softly, coming up beside him. "What was it? The horses?"

He shook his head.

"Drinking?"

"That would be a lot of liquor, baby."

He looked down at her and there was a mixture of hurt and tenderness and shame in his eyes. The walls of her heart seemed to lock together, crushing out the warmth that had risen to her breasts, turning everything to dry, brittle ice. The ice seemed to crunch in there and melt, filling her whole body with the cold. Her eyes, upturned to him, asked him the only question there was left to ask.

"You are so right," he said, quietly. His hands came out and up and touched her shoulders, digging into the flesh. "You know and I know."

She nodded, not trusting her voice.

"It's so very hard for me to tell you, Della. That's why I wanted to talk to you that night. I didn't want to hurt you. And now I have—in many ways."

"Yes," she said.

"I'm sorry as hell."

"Who is she?" The words came out hard and uneven.

"Don't you know?"

And in that moment she did know. The knowledge came to her in a sweeping, jumbled wave and she hated herself for not having known before.

"I thought your wife was getting a divorce," was all she could say.

He turned and walked to the radio, saw that she had turned it off, and left it alone.

"That's what I wanted to tell you, that night. Shirley called me that afternoon, from Reno. She said she'd been thinking it over and that she didn't really want a divorce. She said—"

"That they'd moved the shingle pile?" Della flung at

him.

"Baby, I wouldn't say that again." A little nerve twitched at the side of his jaw, moving the scar. "We all make mistakes. Plenty of them. She made a mistake with Hank—because of me, because Hank was such a big slob and he wanted it like that. I made a mistake of drinking too much and not getting Shirley out of there. And I made another mistake when I came up here with you. I—"

"You made a mistake!" She was shaking all over now. "You made a mistake! For Pete's sake what do you think I made?"

"She wants to come back," he said calmly. "I want her back."

"How romantic!"

"It's as simple as that, Della. I told her—Della, I told her that I'd been doing so good, hoping that she'd come back, that I'd bought this place in the country where we could live and I could farm. That's what I needed the money for. I had a chance to buy this farm, and she was coming back and I'd told her that I already had it. I had to do something about getting the place. I've always wanted to farm, Della."

"You'll get all the farming you want," she assured him. "And more. They'll put a striped suit on you and run you up and down potato rows. We'll find out how much you like farming."

"Don't be too sure of that, baby."

"I'll send you a cultivator for Christmas," she said, remembering how it had been back home. "And some stuff to keep the bugs out of your hair when you get out in the hot morning sun in the summer and you start to sweat. Please, Jack! You must have pulled a spoke out of one of your wheels!"

He shook his head.

"The only way I could get this farm was for cash. The owner had another buyer, but it was a building-and-loan thing and the owner wanted the money to settle a judgment against him for an auto accident. I've put in for a loan and I'm going to get it. And as soon as it goes through—the search of the deed, and the papers are drawn up and signed—you're going to get your money. Every cent of it, baby. What belongs to you. You're going to get it all."

"All right."

He was there, next to her, but she couldn't touch him because he was really so far away, standing there like some stranger she didn't know, a man who had come into her life and passed out into the night.

"That's the way it's going to be, Della. In a few days you'll have it. Then you can square things all around. We'll break up Shinglers, Incorporated. I'll resign from Wyandot, and we'll forget the whole thing. How about it, baby?"

Now he was crawling, now he was promising, trying to turn this nightmare into a day dream. He was a fool!

"It isn't quite as easy as that," she said, giving it to him straight. "You forged my name. That's against the law. When Mr. Gordon gets here to question me about this mess, he's getting all the facts. That check is down at the bank; they know it isn't my signature, and the whole thing is going to land right in your lap. When they get finished with you, you can settle down to your farming."

He laughed at her, low and deep, and the laugh cut everything else away from them, mocking the nights they had shared, making a farce of all that had been theirs for such a short time.

"I committed no forgery, baby. When we formed our corporation, we each signed a power of attorney. It was a pretty conclusive paper, if you'll recall. While it wasn't intended to be used in conducting Wyandot's business, it didn't say anything against that, and I think a good lawyer would make it stick. It's enough to make the company stop and think before they do anything about it. Besides, they have their money. You saw to that, baby."

"Damn you!" she shouted. She hated him, the way he stood and the way he winked at her, because he was so right and there wasn't a thing she could do about it.

"If you put the finger on me," he said, "you'll expose yourself."

She said nothing, fighting back the tears that grew hot behind her closed eyes.

"You'd lose this swell job you've got, baby. You'd cut the plank right out from under your feet. You wouldn't want to do that, would you?"

She shook her head, turning away from him.

"So you won't say anything, baby. You'll just tell the company that you don't know what happened. You'll let them dig their own sand to find out what it was. They don't want anything except the money, and they've got that. You say just one word about me and I'll throw this Shinglers' deal into their face. Then we'll see who gets a job farming first."

"Damn you!" she kept saying over and over. "Oh, damn you!"

She saw him cross the room and take his coat from the back of a chair. He put the coat on, pulled a small raveling loose from the dark blue material, dropped it on the floor and then buttoned the coat neatly.

"You never wanted anything from me except money, baby. When you get this wad that'll be the end of it."

"That's not true, Jack."

"Why try to flatter me, baby?"

"You never had a nickel to your name," she said. "Not a nickel."

"But I could sell—that's the same thing. All the time I thought I was using you, you were twisting me around like a screw in a cork. You had me going, baby. I love my wife and I've been with plenty of women, but I'll give you credit—you've got what it takes to make a man want to die in the same bed with you. You've been in heat ever since I met you, baby."

She hardly realized that her hand was on the ash tray, lifting it, her arm curving back past her shoulder. Then her arm jerked forward and a sharp pain stabbed at her elbow as her empty hand followed through with the motion. She saw Jack throw his body to one side, heard the heavy glass object thud against the wooden door frame.

"Get out of here, you son-of-a-bitch!" she screamed as he flung the door open. "You dirty bastard!"

And then he was gone and she was huddled there on the davenport, alone and crying and terrified. She wished that the ash tray had hit him a wallop. No, she shouldn't wish that because it might have killed him and he'd caused her enough trouble already. She guessed that he didn't much care about the trouble he'd brought to her, and knowing that he felt like that made her feel even worse. She had made such a wonderful success of everything and now she was on the verge of losing it. That auditor had suspected her—she could tell by the way he'd looked at her, the way he'd acted when he'd told her that the office would send Mr. Roger Gordon down to go over things more thoroughly.

It was a stinking shame.

She lay there for a long time, crying, and the pillow with the Dutch windmill on it darkened with her tears. It was the pillow that Jack had won for her pitching baseballs at some milk bottles at a carnival late the past fall. She remembered about that now and she got up and slammed the pillow across the room. It hit the wall and dropped down out of sight behind a chair. Out of sight, she thought, just like Jack. Not worth the feathers it had taken to stuff either one of them.

She went over to the window and looked out, swearing a little when she saw that the liquor store on the corner was closed. The deepness of the night hung over Bolton and pretty soon morning would come and tomorrow would be here. The kids would run along the streets, trying to keep warm on their way to school, and the usual drunk would come staggering along, not giving a hoot about the ice where the power company's drain pipe overflowed and froze across the sidewalk and where a lot of sober people had cracked their skulls. And Della would go out and back her car out of the heated garage—ten dollars a month and all the free looks the owner could get when a girl got into her car. She'd probably drive straight down to the office, skipping coffee, wishing to heaven that Mr. Gordon would get there and get it over with.

Her hands went down over her body, pressing into the flesh that was soft and full of promise. She tried to think of Mr. Roger Gordon and the last time she'd seen him. By the time she turned away from the window she was no longer crying. Her smile was moist and confident, just thinking about Mr. Gordon and how she'd handle him.

As she walked into the bedroom she wondered if she could pick up a pair of pajamas for Mr. Gordon to wear— or perhaps he preferred to sleep in the raw.

16

Mr. Roger Gordon arrived late on Thursday afternoon. It had started to snow earlier in the day and outside of the Wyandot office it had piled up in little drifts. When he came in, his coat glistened in the glare of the office light. Della had been sitting near the window, looking out and watching the snow, thinking that maybe he wouldn't get there, that she might as well close up and go down to the bar on the next block where the lights were warm and soft and the drinks good, where the bartender was always eating ice cream out of a paper container.

"Hello, Mr. Gordon," she said, getting up and giving him a big smile. The last time she had called him Roger. She'd do it again, a little later.

She went over and held out her hand. His fingers were cold and soft.

"Hello, Della," he said. "How are you?"

He took off his coat and hung it on the coat rack. The click of Miss Carlson's typewriter was the only sound in the room. She still wore a bandage on her leg; it wasn't a very neat bandage, just a piece of cloth wound around and held in place by her rayon stocking.

"Awful driving," Mr. Gordon said. "That mountain coming into town is like a piece of greased board."

"I banged up the fender on my car this morning," she said.

"You've got a new car?"

"Yes."

"That's bad, all right. You bang up one of those new fenders and you almost have to get a whole new body."

Actually, she had knocked hell out of the front of the car. She still couldn't figure out how it had happened. It had been on the way to work and she had been driving slowly. Then she had seen Jack on the other side of the street. At first, she hadn't seen Shirley, because of the snow and they had been fooling around, tossing some snow at one another like a couple of kids on their third date. For just a moment the tears had come up into her eyes, blurring together with the snow, but it had lasted just long enough for it to happen. The tree had been right there waiting for her and the car hadn't budged it an inch.

"Yes," Mr. Gordon said, lighting a cigar about as long as a broom handle. "This is an awful day. My wife didn't want me to make the trip."

She hoped that they'd get finished kicking the weather around pretty soon and get down to the meat of things.

"I didn't want to come either," Mr. Gordon went on,

belching smoke. Della thought that his glance was somewhat sharp. "But I had to. There's a board meeting next week and this was the only open time before then. I'd hoped to get down here earlier and take care of things and drive right back. But in view of the weather, I think I'd better call Mrs. Gordon and tell her I'll plan to stay all night."

Of course, Della thought, the old fool was going to stay all night. Probably he'd had it in his mind right along. A man as old as Mr. Gordon who had once had from Della what he thought he'd had would go back to the well as often as possible. And he'd keep going back as long as he could get the lid off.

Mr. Gordon made his phone call, mumbled something about dearie to the old bag on the other end a couple of times, threw a kiss that sounded more like a grunt and hung up. He took Della by the arm and led her into her office, carefully, like a father walking down the aisle with a daughter who was about to become a bride.

"Well, Della," he said.

"Yes," she said. "Well."

She sat down on the davenport, her body low and straight out in front of him. Her legs, she thought, had never looked better. She got the impression that he was making up his own mind about that.

"I left the auditor's report out in the car," he said, staring at the chewed end of his cigar. "I didn't bother to bring it in, because I've digested most of it and it doesn't tell too much that's conclusive anyway. I'd much prefer to talk to you on a—shall we say—man to woman basis?"

Della's laugh was low and intimate.

"You express yourself so well," she said.

"I don't know just how to go about this, Della. I was awfully shocked when the auditing department threw this thing at me. I hate any kind of unpleasantness."

"I do, too."

"You must know the reason for my visit, don't you?"

"Well, he said you might come. He said he'd have to report right back to the office that I'd—balled things up a little bit. I had the feeling that he thought that you could straighten it out all right."

"Yes." Mr. Gordon chewed on the cigar some more and when he finished that he dropped it into the wastebasket. "Unfortunately, Della, it doesn't make much difference what he thinks or what I think. There are certain things which appear in his report which are not at all—favorable. It's my job, being in charge of personnel, to investigate these situations and render a decision—a decision which is fair to the employee, to the company, and which is acceptable to our board of directors. I must, at all times, take into consideration the human equation which exists in matters of this type. I'm sure that you'll understand that my job is, at times, a most unpleasant one."

"You have a tremendous responsibility, Mr. Gordon."

"That's the way I look at it."

He sat down in the chair behind Della's desk, his back very erect, his face trying to look stern. Della snuggled a little deeper into the soft cushions on the davenport. Things, she decided, were not going the way they should. She wanted him to forget for a moment that he was such a big wheel in the company, otherwise he might start thinking of the gold watch he'd be getting in another few years, the good things that his high salary bought for him. Once he started thinking like that she'd get caught in his main spring and that might be the end of it for her.

"I wish I felt better," Della said, yawning sleepily. "I wish I didn't feel tired and so all dragged out. Honest, Mr. Gordon, I've been sitting here ever since that man left, almost, trying to figure out what happened."

He was getting himself a good look at the rise and fall of her breasts.

"I'm sorry that you worried so much, Della."

"But I couldn't help it, Mr. Gordon! When I think of the mess I have made—"

"There must be some reason," he said.

"Well, yes, but I couldn't find out what it was. Not right away. I—I've just kept at it until I'm ready to drop. And every minute I thought that you'd come. Every minute I prayed that you'd come through that door, because I knew that my troubles would be over then. I know you must be awfully smart on things like this." She gave him a big smile and drove it at him again. "You must be terribly bright, Mr. Gordon."

"Well—" He shifted his weight to a more relaxed position in the chair. "Well, now, Della, of course I want to help you if I can. There isn't an awful lot to it. There's just the matter of that check. It just seems to me—"

"Oh, I'm so glad that you feel that way about it!" she exclaimed, giving him a little peek above her knees. "I was so worried that you might be mean and gruff with me—just because there's a little error. That's mostly what's made me feel so miserable. I was worried about how you might feel. After all, you're the one who had confidence in me, the one who gave me this job. I want to do everything you want me to do, Mr. Gordon, and I want to do it right."

There was a bedroom huskiness to her voice that dug down under his thick business shell and promised him big dividends to come.

"That's nice," he said.

"I guess I couldn't have stood it another day, if you hadn't come, Mr. Gordon. I guess I would have called you, just to talk with you, just to get some kind of assurance that you don't think I'm a complete flop. I've been thinking—well, something like this could happen to almost anybody."

"Yes," he agreed. "I suppose it could."

"That's just how I've been trying to think of it, Mr.

Gordon. But it's been difficult. I want so much to do a good job for you, for Wyandot—"

"You have, Della."

"—and myself, of course. I got myself sick just thinking about all this trouble."

"That auditor shouldn't have upset you so much."

"Oh, he was just doing his job, I guess."

"He must have made it pretty difficult for you," Mr. Gordon said. "I'll talk to that young man when I get back to the office."

"Don't do that, please," Della said. She didn't want any more trouble with that guy. "We can straighten it out and everything will be fine. Besides, Mr. Gordon, I know all about that check now. I have the answer to it."

"You have"

"Oh, yes. And it's terrible. Awful!" She sighed and smiled wistfully. "I've been such a dupe, Mr. Gordon."

"I'm afraid I don't understand."

"I know you're going to be surprised, too." She let that hang just long enough so that he'd know that things were going to be all right again, and then she said, listlessly, "But since I don't feel up to par today and since you're staying over tonight, maybe you'd just as soon tackle it first thing in the morning. If we start out feeling good and fresh—I know you must be just dead after your hard drive up here—why, it wouldn't take us any time at all."

This had to be the way that she'd do it. She couldn't very well tell him about Jack, and she certainly couldn't hang it onto Miss Carlson while the old gal was out there in the office, right within shouting distance. She'd wait until morning, get down to the bank early and destroy the check—until now she'd forgotten about Jack's endorsement on it—and then she'd give Miss Carlson a ring on the phone and tell her that she was giving her the axe, that she'd send her two weeks pay and that she should stay home with her cats where she belonged. When Mr.

Gordon got down to the office she'd be alone with him and she'd tell him that Miss Carlson had quit, rather than get fired, and she'd spin him a yarn like he'd never heard before. After a night's play in the hay he ought to go for that one like a bull chasing a two year old heifer.

She needn't have worried—it didn't take him much time to think that one over.

"I guess that would be all right," he said, loosening his tie. "It's almost five now and I'm a little tired. Maybe I ought to be tired—I'm not as young as I used to be."

He was shopping for a compliment, so she sold him one.

"You're not so old," she said, giving him a wink. "Why, you're not old at all, Mr. Gordon."

The way he looked at her, she knew that he was trying to capture that night in the hotel room again, not having much luck and hating himself because things like that just faded away.

"What about dinner?" he asked, getting up out of the chair. "I know it's rather early, but I've got to look around and find a room for the night and I thought maybe we could have a couple of drinks and something to eat while I was at it."

"Oh, I don't know," Della said, yawning. "I just feel sort of—blah! Getting dressed for dinner seems like too much effort."

"I've got to get a room, anyway."

"Well, you don't have to hurry on that. I can always fix you up with that."

The way he tried to keep his smile back, she knew he liked what she'd said.

"You wouldn't have to get dressed for dinner," Mr. Gordon said. "Nothing fancy, I mean. We can go to some small place. Just a meal."

"It's a terrible night to go out and get stuck in the snow," she said.

"I wouldn't want to do that."

"There's one thing that we could do," she said, crossing her legs so he'd get an idea of what the rest of her looked like. "Why don't we just have a light dinner up at my apartment? It'd give me a chance to brush up on my cooking."

He didn't have to think that one over very long either.

"That sounds like a better idea," he said. She got up and he didn't miss a movement. "Much better, Della."

They left Miss Carlson to lock the office for the night and they went out through the snow to his car. She had left her own car in the garage that morning and the man down there had told her that it would be almost a week before they got the dents from the tree pried out of it.

"Storm's getting worse," he said.

Someone had shoveled the sidewalk, piling the fluffy white against the car door. Della tried to open it a couple of times, gave up and went around and slid in from the driver's side.

The rear wheels screamed in the snow as Mr. Gordon jumped up and down on the gas.

"Guess we're stuck already," he said.

"Wait a minute," Della told him. "Just pull your emergency on a little and then give her the gas in low, real slow."

"Like this?"

"Yes."

"I'll try it." The big car moved out into the street, picking up traction. "That was okay," he said, grinning at her. "I'd have been there for hours."

"Just a little trick," she said.

Up on the banks of the Willowkill a person either knew those things or stayed snowed in half of the winter. Sometimes the town crews plowed the roads and sometimes they didn't. It all depended on whether or not it was payday and which bar they were headed for when they put the plows down. Along the Willowkill nobody gave much of a damn. In the winter there wasn't any place to go and nothing to do after getting there.

"It's a hell of a night," Mr. Gordon said, peering ahead into the driving white.

"It certainly is."

"There's just one other thing I want to ask you about," he said. "Then we won't talk business until tomorrow. What about Jack Bishop? He wired in his resignation and I was wondering about that. He was a pretty good man, wasn't he?"

"He wanted to become a farmer," she said. "I guess he bought himself a farm."

"I thought it must be something like that."

You're damned right it was something like that, Della thought angrily. He'd been going so fast into the farming business the last time she'd seen him that she hadn't gotten a good look at him for dollar bills. He'd made a point, that day he'd come into the office, of showing her the money and then standing there grinning while she'd had to count those singles. Three thousand of them. And then she'd asked him about the other money from Shinglers, Incorporated.

He'd asked her what money? Was she crazy? Had she been drinking? Wasn't it enough that the corporation had been dissolved, that everything belonging to Shinglers was now her property? How much did she want, anyway? Didn't she have enough? Sure, she had enough. She had plenty. More than she knew what to do with. She had two carpenters who didn't have any work, a checkbook without a balance and not enough material on hand to shingle a one story chicken coop.

The big car skidded a couple of times as Mr. Gordon followed her directions and turned in at a side street. The snow was deeper here, stacked in sharp, irregular drifts that were taking on hard surfaces from the rising whip of the wind and the patter of rain. After he stopped the car she got out, feeling the snow cold around her ankles, ducking her head against the sting of the sleet that nicked her face and hands. Mr. Gordon came around the car and got hold of her arm. He was breathing heavily as they trudged up the walk and went stamping into the warm hall. Della installed Mr. Gordon in the living room with a couple of magazines, a tall rye and soda and then went into the bedroom to change. She put on a blue, form fitting dress which accentuated the blonde of her hair, and a pair of low heeled shoes with narrow straps that directed attention to her slim ankles. She started to go out of the room, stopped, took off the shoes and her stockings and put on a pair of fluffy edged slippers. Then she went out to the kitchen, humming softly.

They ate the steak and French fries and lettuce and tomato salad in the living room on a card table that threatened to collapse at almost any moment. Mr. Gordon attacked the steak with the ferocity of a starved bear, ate the French fries with his fingers and pronounced the tomatoes as being better than if they were out of a garden. Della wondered, silently, where the hell he thought they'd been grown. She ate almost mechanically, since she seemed to have no appetite whatsoever.

Mr. Gordon was leaning back in his chair picking his teeth when Della realized what was wrong with her. She had not been lying to him that afternoon. She felt like hell.

"I'm sorry," she said, "but I'm afraid I don't have any dessert."

"After a meal like that?"

"We could go down to the corner and get something. They make good cake down there."

"I've got a better idea than that," he said. "I've got a couple of bottles down in the car. What say we just drink our dessert?"

Maybe that was what she needed, something strong and harsh to numb the anxiety of these last few days. Somehow, she had to forget, just for a little while, that there were such things as Wyandot, money, Jack—or this old guy who sat across from her and who now had just one thing on his mind.

"If you don't have another idea all night," she said, "that one will be good enough for me."

He stood up and grinned down at her. She could see that he had other ideas.

"I'll be right back," he said.

While he was gone she cleaned away the dishes and stacked them on the drainboard in the kitchen. Pretty soon he came in, shaking the snow out of his gray hair, and set the two bottles of Old Forester by the dirty dishes. Then he helped her get the cubes out of the ice tray, stood there close behind her, blowing down the back of her neck, as she ran some more water into the tray.

"I'll take the drinks in," he said.

"Okay."

"Maybe we should do the dishes."

"There's plenty of time for that."

"Sure," he said. "Later."

He poured the drinks down over the ice and she noticed that he put two shots in one of them. He went out through the doorway whistling. She put the tray back in the ice box and followed him out to the living room. He had turned all the lights out except one and he had their drinks over by the davenport.

"Luck," he said.

The liquor burned in her throat, taking her breath away. She felt the warmth spreading through her and she began to feel better. She was glad that he had given her the one with the double jolt.

They had some more drinks and after a while they rolled back the rug, turned up the radio and danced very slowly in the small space. They didn't need much room. He held her so tight that they could have done the same thing in a closet.

A news broadcast came on and they drank some more. When that went off the music came back, low and dreamy. Roger Gordon got hold of her and started pushing her around again. When they got over by the light he just stood still, holding her, and then reached out and turned the light off. When his hand came back he put it on one of her breasts.

"Don't, please!"

He took his hand away, reached up and started unbuttoning her dress. She could hear him breathing hard, smell the sweat of his body, see his face twisted in the half-light.

"Damn it!" he kept whispering. "Damn it!"

He slipped the dress down over her shoulders, fumbled for the hook on her brassiere. She heard the cloth rip as he tore it loose. Then both of his hands were up there, fondling her.

"Lord! What a pair!"

He bent and kissed her and then his hand went exploring farther, as she tried to move away, feeling sick, knowing that it shouldn't be like this.

She closed her eyes but it didn't do any good. She seemed to be spinning. He was half-dragging her toward the davenport. She tried to walk, but she couldn't. She felt so weak —so damned weak.

He wanted her and she'd have to let him have her. He was an awful man, but it was the only possible way now. She'd have to let him do it. But she didn't want him to do it. She didn't.

"Della! Della, are you all right?"

His voice wasn't at all distinct and it was cold in the room, but there seemed to be more light and that was something. The spinning had stopped and she opened her eyes. The lamp above the davenport was glowing softly and she blinked at it a couple of times. She tried to roll over but there was a blanket around her and that was stuck in between the cushions. When she moved, the spinning started again. She kept her eyes open, swallowing hard.

"Della?"

"Yes."

His face was there above her and she could see the fear in his eyes.

"You all right?"

"Why, sure."

"I—Della, I think maybe I'd better go and let you rest. You need to—relax."

She nodded her head stupidly. He went over and got his hat and coat and put them on. She wanted to get up and go to him and tell him to stay, but she couldn't seem to do a thing about it. She was so miserably weak and, besides, there was always tomorrow.

"I hope you'll feel better in the morning," he said.

"Thanks."

He wasn't worried about her. He was just concerned about getting out of that apartment as fast as he could pull the door open.

"Good night."

"Good night—Roger."

The door hissed closed behind him. She heard his heels on the stairs, descending rapidly. He was in a great deal of hurry. Just thinking about that caused her to laugh and cry in long, uneven sobs. He didn't have to rush like that. There was no reason for him to be afraid. He could have hung around and got what he wanted. He could have stayed as long as he wished. There was no reason for him to run like that. There was plenty of time. Lots of time.

Hell, the way she had it figured, it would be at least seven months before this kid would be born.

17

The shadows of the night crept across Bolton, bringing with it the end of the day and all that it had been for Della Banners.

She sat alone in her office where she had experienced no difficulty at all making plans during the past, but where now she found it impossible to comprehend her doubtful future. The cellophane had cracked, exposing her and leaving her very much alone; the cellophane was cloudy now, not bright and shiny like it had been. Things were really up in the air.

The phone started ringing, but she didn't answer it. She was tired of answering it. It had been screaming in her ears all day. First it had been Miss Carlson, crying; then the mechanic at the garage; after that it was Miss Carlson again, several times, crying some more and getting mad and hollering her head off. She was sick of Miss Carlson.

She was glad that she'd fired her, even though it hadn't done any good.

The man had called her about the lease on the apartment, but she'd hung up on him, not wanting to talk about it, because after this shuffle she'd be lucky if she could pay the light bills. She didn't want to talk to anybody. Yes, she did. She wanted to talk to one person—just one. But what she had to say to him couldn't be said over the phone. She knew that. She'd tried to call him, tried to say it. And he'd cut her off, every time, leaving nothing but the dead, silence of the telephone wires.

She lit a cigarette and let her thoughts linger for a few moments on the events which had preceded Mr. Gordon's departure. He'd been in a sour mood when he'd reached the office that morning. He'd had quite a time finding a room at the hotel and the one which they'd assigned him hadn't had any running water, the steam had been off most of the night, and the blankets on the bed had been too short. In addition to all of those things, Della supposed that he'd been upset about her inadequacies of the night before. Had she dared tell him the truth about it, he'd have realized that she felt much worse about it than he did, and with greater reason.

Lord, she thought, a baby! She'd wondered about it last month, around the first, but she'd been so busy that she'd almost forgotten about it. Besides, things had been going good then and she hadn't worried much about it. But she supposed that she'd better start doing some high-class worrying about it right away. Maybe she could find a doctor—no, she wouldn't do that. That was funny. She'd told Miss Dolan to do that and now the thought of doing it herself revolted her. She wouldn't ever do that. More than likely she'd reached the world through some sort of an accident and she wasn't going to hold anybody else up just because she was faced with the same thing.

She wondered if it would be a boy or a girl. If it were a girl, would she look like her mother? If it were a boy— well, she didn't want any son of hers to look like Jack. Anyway, she didn't want him to be like Jack. Did she want him—or her—to be like either one of them? For Pete's sake, what kind of a choice did the poor kid have?

She crushed out the cigarette and some of the ash stuck to her thumb, burning sharply. She got up from the desk and walked over to the window. She didn't know why she did that. There wasn't anything out there to see. There was just the blank wall of the building next door. She put her hands on her stomach and felt the round, soft fullness of it. The baby was down there! She wondered why she hadn't suspected this before. She'd even been silly enough to buy a couple of girdles, thinking they might help her. That certainly had been stupid! What she had, no girdle would help.

She speculated as to whether or not Mr. Gordon had guessed her condition. He had suspected everything else about her. She knew that the dodge about Miss Carlson having made out the check hadn't gone over. He hadn't been able to understand why the old lady had done it, why Della hadn't safeguarded the check and not left it around where it could be destroyed. He'd gone through the books, hardly listening to her rambling explanations, and she'd known; even before he'd left that afternoon, that he'd made up his mind about her.

She turned away from the window, crossed the room and shrugged into her fur coat. She snapped out the light and walked out through the darkened outer office. A swirl of snow greeted her as she opened the door and went out into the night.

What the hell, she thought. She still had some money, didn't she? After she paid off the bank—and who said she was going to do that?—she'd have about eleven hundred left, the car free and clear, and a lot of fancy clothes that she wouldn't be able to get into until sometime next year. Lord, wasn't she lucky?

Friday night. Friday night and she'd be canned before the end of the week. Things were shot. Her car was in the garage, there was a foot of snow on the ground and she was higher than a kite in a hurricane.

She picked her way carefully between the piles of snow. She had to be careful now. She mustn't fall down. There were two of them out there in this storm. She had to take care of Jack's kid. He'd want her to do that. Yeah! She laughed and the laugh was killed by the rush of the wind. Jack wouldn't mind. Not at all.

They'd both said the same thing, that weekend they'd spent in the office. They'd both said that it would be all right if it turned out like this. But that had been then, before things changed, when they only said words to each other and the words didn't mean very much. But now it was later and all that they'd had was gone—and the words still didn't have any meaning. A bitch in heat, he'd said. He was a fine one to talk. He'd been like a stud horse at a county fair. Who the hell did he think he was kidding?

She turned up the sidewalk to the gray shingled house where Jack now had his room. The frost on the front steps crunched under her feet, and in the little storm shelter around the door she paused to get her breath. It seemed like hours that she waited there, but it wasn't long because when she got to the head of the steps she was breathing so hard that she could hardly hear the sound of her knock over the moan of the radio inside.

The music stopped and for a moment there was just the sound of the wind outside and of footsteps shuffling across a floor. Then the door yawned open and she stood in the bright light, the snow melting on the long hairs of her coat and her eyes large and just a little frightened at seeing him again.

"Hello, Jack."

He stepped back as though she had struck him.

"I said hello."

"I heard you the first time." His face looked pained and tired.

"Well?"

"I don't know what you're doing here, Della."

"I'd like to talk to you," she said, feeling a surprising calm settle over her. "You wouldn't talk to me on the phone."

"There isn't anything for us to talk about."

"We've got plenty to talk about."

Shirley's tall dark form appeared from behind Jack, then stood there beside him. Della's hard stare never wavered from Jack's face.

"All right," he said, moving to one side.

"She's not coming in here!" Shirley said. She clung to her husband's arm. "Please, darling, send her away!"

But Della was already inside the room. It was a small place, with a couple of chairs, a desk and a Murphy bed. In one corner there was a white porcelain sink and a little cupboard and an electric plate. The smell of bacon and eggs still hung in the room and two empty plates with bits of toast on them sat on a tray on top of the radio.

"You sure have your nerve to come here," Shirley said.

"I've got something," Della agreed.

Shirley went over and poked at the plates. She carried them to the sink and threw them in. It sounded as if one of them broke, with the small pieces rattling down into the gooseneck of the drain.

"See here," Jack said, looking uncomfortable as Della removed her coat. "We straightened everything out before. I sent in my resignation the other day."

"Jack's getting out of the roofing business," Shirley said.

Della just stood there, a slight smile pulling at her lips, letting the full effect of her presence reach them, confuse and annoy them. Jack shrugged his shoulders, picked up a paper from the back of one of the chairs and threw it down again. Shirley turned on the water, shut it off quickly, and wheeled to face Della.

"You're wasting your time coming here, Miss Banners."

"I'm the last one to deny that."

"We're starting all over again," Shirley said, looking at Jack. "We've both made mistakes and we know it. We're forgetting the past. I know about you and Jack. I don't hate you. It was one of those things. It happened and it's over with."

"Well, it isn't over with."

"I tell you it is!"

"Shut up, both of you!" Jack shouted. He frowned at Della. "I don't know why you came here. Just like Shirley says, we've got everything straightened out and we're going to keep it that way."

"That's fine. Congratulations."

"If you believed that, you wouldn't be here. You'd leave us alone." He looked at his wife and she smiled back at him. "You can't understand what's gone on inside of me, Della."

"I guess not."

"You'll never know the hell I went through, doing the things I didn't want to do, hating myself because I did them, not able to stop because it didn't seem to matter."

"Sure. I was twisting your arm all the time."

He was still looking at his wife, not hearing a thing that she said.

"Now we've got this farm and as soon as the weather gets good we're going to move out there and get started. We've got a long ways to go and we know it's going to be hard—but we're going to work and we're going to get there."

"Maybe you'd like some company?" Della inquired.

"I don't think I get you," Jack said, slowly, turning to her.

"I suppose I'll have to draw you a picture," she said. "Why do you think I'd bother coming here? To wish you two luck?"

The silence in the room became tense and electric. Della saw the color drain from Shirley's face, her teeth bite down hard on her lower lip, the dark eyes take on a peculiar, misty shine. Jack looked from one girl to the other and Della felt herself trembling inside, her knees growing weak, heard the dull roar crowding up into her head.

"Oh, no!" Shirley gasped. "Oh, no! Not that!"

She came to her husband in a rush, burying her head against his chest, seeking comfort and safety. Something tore at her body, shaking her. Jack held her close, looking straight ahead, his fingers digging down into her arms.

Della stood there, watching them, torn by a series of conflicting emotions. She wanted to go to this girl, to tell her not to worry, to help her accept this nightmare that had now become a part of their lives. And she wanted to drive her from the room, out of Jack's life, so that she could have Jack for herself. That way, they could have a home together and they would be able to give this baby all of the things that a baby might want and need. And then, in a rising cartwheel of thoughts, she hated Jack, his excuses, his plans for the future, everything that was a part of him. She hated herself. She did not hate herself for what she had done or what had happened. She was not particularly ashamed of her pregnancy—a lot of good girls forgot to watch the calendar. The thing which cried out to her was her own stupidity. If she'd had an ounce of sense in her head she'd have been caught—if she was to be caught at all—by someone who could make the trouble worthwhile.

"Are you sure?" Jack demanded, his voice husky. "Della, are you positive?"

She nodded.

"You could be wrong."

"I'll never be more pregnant," she said.

"Maybe it wasn't you," Shirley said hopefully, glancing up at her husband.

His eyes took on a sudden, strange gleam.

"Yeah," he said, taking his arms from around her. "That's right. Maybe it wasn't me."

"It's you all right," Della said.

"How do I know? How do I know—that you know?"

Her throat was tight and dry.

"I know all right," she said, a trifle desperately. "And so do you, damn you! You think I'm glad it happened? You think I planned this?"

He looked at her for a long moment.

"You'd plan anything to get what you wanted," he said. "There isn't anything you wouldn't do."

"Maybe you're right, Jack. After sleeping with you I might do almost anything."

"Jack!" Shirley's face was white. "You told me that you didn't!"

"Of course I didn't," he said.

Della could hear and feel the thud and pound of her heart. She saw that apartment again, the bedroom, and she could almost feel his hands on her, seeking her, thrilling her to the limits of her passion. His whispered pleas and promises came plunging at her in a growing, haunting torrent.

"You damned liar!" she hurled at him.

"Now, Della, please—"

"Look at me!" she challenged him. "Look at me and say that!"

He glanced at his wife and then at Della. His eyes were steady and wide open.

"I never did," he said. "I never even wanted to."

"I suppose you never undressed me?"

"No!"

"Or told me that the desk in the office was the best place of all, because you could—"

"Stop it!" Shirley moaned, covering her face with her hands. "Oh, don't!"

"You tramp!" Jack yelled at her. "You dirty little tramp!"

She felt her fingernails cut into his face, saw the blood, red and dripping on her hand. Viciously she lashed out and struck him again.

His hands, powerful and hot, closed on her wrists. The pain drove up her arms to her shoulders, to her neck, shooting across her head in stinging waves. Her body lurched blindly, trying to escape him. Tears of pain and anger and frustration clouded her sight and from somewhere within she heard her voice pleading with him, begging him.

"Don't, Jack! No! Oh—I can't—"

Her voice ended in a half sob, half scream as he struck her hard across the side of the face. She felt herself reeling, stumbling, and then the soft goodness of the bed. Her tears were hot and wet on her cheeks, and she could taste the salt and the blood in her mouth. She sat up slowly and she saw that he was there, standing over her, his face twisted and gray.

"I'm sorry," she said, willing to say almost anything that would end this and let her get out of that room. "I just forgot myself."

"You forgot a lot of things, baby."

Don't call me baby, she thought. Don't call me baby when it means so little and you hate me so much.

"I didn't mean to say that," she said, trying to get up.

"You filthy bitch!" he sneered, holding her there on the bed. "So, all right, I slept with you. You wanted me to, though, didn't you? Sure you did. That was the only way that you could get what you wanted. It's the only way you'll ever get what you want."

She stared back at him, hurt and numb.

"You're worse than a tramp, Della. A tramp charges for what she gives, and if you're not satisfied you don't go back to her again. You give something and you keep on demanding. You're not even honest enough to put a price on what you've got."

"Oh, Jack, Jack, don't say that!"

"Whore!" he shouted. "Whore!"

Slowly, deliberately, Della got to her feet. She looked up at him and laughed. Then she looked at Shirley and laughed again. Very carefully she straightened her skirt, turned to glance over her shoulder to see if the seams of her stockings were straight. Her coat had fallen on the floor, so she picked that up and slipped into it.

"I wasn't going to cause you any trouble," Della told Jack. "I just wanted you to know, so that you could help me make things right. I guess you don't see it that way. Okay. You've got a lot of smart answers, telling me what I am and what's wrong with me, but there's only one way

I could get like this. You had your fun, Jack, and, by heaven, you're going to pay for it!"

He started to say something, but the effort seemed to be too great and he just stood there, his shoulders drooping, shaking his head.

"I wish that you'd leave," Shirley said.

"Don't worry. I'm going."

"Jack will get in touch with you."

Della went over to the door and pulled it wide open. She hesitated there for a moment, buttoning her coat, feeling that this was the end of something important, something that would be with her for a long time to come.

"You needn't come back, Miss Banners."

She didn't say anything, only shut her eyes and tried to keep from crying and to get the coat buttoned. The button had always stuck and she wanted to rip it off, but she didn't have the strength to do it. She wondered if she could walk and she tried it, slowly, blinking her eyes to get the tears out of the way.

She felt a rush of air and she knew that the door was closing on her fast, too fast, but she couldn't do very much about it.

The door struck her, but it didn't seem to hurt very much, just pushed her ahead. She seemed to be dropping down into a great vacuum that didn't require any effort on her part. She heard the scream ringing in her ears, bounding in a shrill echo off the walls. She wished that she could stop making so much noise.

Then the pain shot through her, sucking the air from her lungs, and she felt tired, so terribly tired.

Down at the bottom of the stairs, near the umbrella stand, Della Banners lay in a small, quiet heap of flesh and cloth.

18

It was certainly odd how everything could suddenly be so wonderful and right and peaceful. There were only a couple of things that Della didn't like about it. She had never cared very much for plain white and there was too much of it around her. And the people who insisted on talking to her never came very close, but seemed to stay far away, mumbling, as if they were speaking to her through paper walls.

She felt warm and comfortable, lying there. She knew that she was lying down because her back was getting tired of it and once in a while hurt like hell. She supposed that she was in a bed because it seemed soft, not hard and cold, and no one was trying to push her around any more. It would be nice if she could open her eyes, but that seemed like a lot of effort and she could do that any time she got around to it.

She didn't know how long she had been there—a day, a week, forever. She remembered talking to someone—oh, talking with a lot of people—but it was difficult to get any of it straight. Probably she had been away for a while. She smiled. That was it. She had taken a trip, it didn't matter where, and she had talked to those people. They had been pleasant enough. They hadn't argued with her. Even Jack had been reasonable about it. She smiled again. That's how she knew about the trip. Jack had told her all about it.

"I'm going away," he'd told her. She recalled how his voice had sounded, low and cracked, but it was impossible to remember how he'd looked. "Maybe for a year, maybe two years."

That's an awfully long time, she thought. It would almost seem as though he would get tired of such a long trip.

Two years. Why, he could go around the world a couple of times in one year, and more than that in two. Besides, what was the damn fool going to use for money?

"I won't need any money," he'd told her, when she'd asked him about that. His laugh had annoyed her. "No money required. Not where I'm going. Thanks for fixing it up, baby."

She couldn't remember having done anything for him, and she was pretty sure that she hadn't—or hadn't meant to, anyway. She'd asked him about his wife—that much stood out clear.

"Things will work out for us. Shirley's going to get a job and wait for me—I hope."

Della smiled to herself. Why on earth would anybody in their right mind want to work? There was so much money around that it didn't seem possible that anybody would consider doing it. There had been a man—someone by the name of Jordon, or Gordon, or something like that—who had talked about money, as though there was plenty of it.

"Yes, that's right, Mrs. Banners, the inventory was short, but we expected that. It was just about the check that we had to be sure of. They had a photostat at the bank and we found out about it down there. No, Della didn't owe anything on that. You don't have to worry, Mrs. Banners. Della had enough money to take care of everything. Try to stop worrying about that part of it, won't you?"

Della decided that this was pretty good. There was a lot of money—the man had said so, hadn't he?—and her mother would be all right. She was glad of that. She didn't want her mother to worry. Her mother was getting old and she had a lot of dresses to make for people and maybe they wouldn't pay her. But that was a silly thing to think about. No one would try to stick her mother. As the man had said, there was lots of money around.

This money business confused Della. It didn't seem to

her as though she had any money, but surely it shouldn't be hard to figure out a way of getting her hands on some. Somebody might step up and ask her for some money and then what would she do? Yes, what would she do? And what difference would it make anyway?

Oh, hell, this place was too small, too stuffy and cramped. She wondered how she could go about getting out of there. If she could only find her shoes, her dress and her coat, she could walk right out. And if she could locate her pocketbook, providing there was some money in it, things would be different. If she even had an idea about what was going on that would help a lot.

She stirred a little under the sheet. It shouldn't be too difficult to find a way out. There had been a voice—a strange, deep, patient voice—talking about that very thing.

"The baby is gone, of course. I'm afraid there never was any doubt about that."

So, she reasoned, if a baby could get up and leave, why couldn't she? She could go anywhere a baby could go. But, then, perhaps somebody took him. Or was it a baby girl? Why hadn't the man said something about that? Also, the baby must belong to someone and he hadn't said anything about that, either.

Well, it wasn't her baby. She didn't have any baby. She wasn't married and she was much too smart to get like that without having a husband first. Any girl in her right mind didn't get herself pregnant just for the fun of it. A girl got married and wanted a family and she slept with her husband and it was still fun.

What in hell was the matter with that stupid Jack? He was going on a trip and his wife wasn't going with him. That part was all right, because his wife had no business going—she should stay home and work her head off. But, she, Della, should have been invited. Didn't she belong with Jack? Weren't they two of a kind?

God damn it, Jack, what happened to you?

Somehow, she would have to get things straightened out with Jack. He was so confused about everything and his going away made it even worse. She wished that she knew where he was going. He should have left her an address where she could write. Later on, she'd want to let him know about the baby. Oh, God! She kicked and tossed in the bed, not minding the pain in her back. So there had been a baby! Her baby. Jack's baby. That must have been the baby the man spoke about. And the baby was gone, gone, gone! Where the hell had that kid gone?

Her scream filled the room. The sound of it startled her. She threw her body to the right, bumping into the wall, twisting deeper into the sheets.

That Jack, she thought. What a colossal flop he was. He could sell shingles, and he could live with his wife and he could make another woman pregnant, but other than that he didn't know from nothing. And now he was going away on this trip. That was a good thing, maybe. She didn't feel sorry about it any more. Some day he'd get his ticket punched, good, and then he wouldn't be so smart. Besides, what was the poor jerk going to use for money?

Della smiled wisely. She didn't have to worry about that. She guessed that there was plenty of money. She'd heard the man tell her mother that. It had seemed like a foolish reason for her mother to start bawling.

Other thoughts came to Della, but they were like great drifting clouds on a dark gray horizon, ever moving, always in a hurry, never making much of a pattern. Her mother had done some talking, but she hadn't made much sense, just got things mixed up the way she generally did.

"I never thought I'd see it." Her mother's voice had been far away, fading. Why hadn't she come closer? "All my life I've worked—and wondered. I keep on wondering. Something like this happens and you see how careless you've been. I don't know. I just don't know."

Della's head rolled from side to side on the white pillow.

Her mother must have hurt herself. Maybe she'd rammed one of those needles through her hand. Sure, maybe she'd been stuck with something sharp, something that would hurt for a long while afterward. Her mother ought to stop sewing. Some day she'd get hurt and not get over it right away. If ever.

Well, Della was going to take care of her mother. When she got out of this place her mother wouldn't have anything to worry about any more. She wasn't going to be like her father, making her mother worry, financing things right and left until she couldn't remember where the middle had been. She was going to play it smart. Maybe Jack would go on that trip and maybe he wouldn't. She'd have to talk to him about that. And she'd have to talk with him about the baby. A baby who walked out of a place like this, alone, ought to catch hell. A kid had no right doing things like that on his own. A kid needed somebody with brains who could set him straight on what he should do.

She closed her eyes and shuddered. She wished that the roaring noise in her head would stop. It hadn't been so bad before, but now it was getting louder and it hurt her ears. She felt cold and she was shaking all over and she didn't like it one bit. Maybe she would shake so much that she would hurt herself. Maybe that was what was wrong with her back. There were machines made to shake a girl up and repair her figure, but she didn't require any of that nonsense. All her life people had been telling her that she was stacked. The English teacher had told her, that day up there in the motion picture booth, that she was almost good enough to swap for a jail sentence. A girl had to have something special to make a man talk that way about her.

The thoughts about jail disturbed her. There shouldn't be any such place. Who wanted to spend their time locked up in a little room? How silly could a person get? When a person got tired of things it was time to do as Jack had it planned, take a trip. A long trip—with all expenses paid.

She was getting very tired and she hoped that these people would stop bothering her. She couldn't recognize who they were, but they were people all right, and they kept walking around the room. Maybe they couldn't find any chairs to sit on, but they could at least stand still and not cause so much confusion. It wouldn't be long before she got ready to leave. They should quiet down, because she might want to say something to them before she left.

She wondered about where she might go. She'd have to make up her mind about that. One of the men—had it been that Mr. Gordon?—had said something about the office, but she felt that she wouldn't be interested in going back there again. She'd seen enough of that place.

It was a little difficult for her to understand just what the old farm along the Willowkill had to do with her future, but it was there, crowding around her, trying to find its place in the very important things which she was thinking about. She supposed that the taxes were paid, but if they weren't, she wasn't going to lose any sleep over it. The taxes had been one thing her father hadn't worried about. He'd had some deal with the county supervisor where he could work on the roads in summer, shoveling gravel into the holes, until he'd earned enough credits to get the county clerk off his neck. Della didn't expect that she could make any arrangement like that, but that was just as well because she planned on playing it smart. From here on in, all the way down the line, she'd only do the smart things.

Right now she wished that she was back there on that old farm. Probably there would be a lot of snow to shovel and the furnace would smoke, but those things weren't important. She had to get out of this place and back there as quickly as possible. That was the first thing for her to do, the start in a series of smart moves that she was going to make. After that she would get around to taking care of Roy. Just thinking about him made her laugh. That would be the smartest move of all, getting things settled with him. Roy was all right. He was a good guy. And he was dumb.

She tried to get up, but her back hurt and the sheet seemed to be very heavy. Yet it shouldn't be difficult to get out of this place, because she certainly could go where a baby could go. And the man with the deep voice knew that she had this in mind, and he was talking about it to her mother.

"Della is just going away on a long trip, Mrs. Banners. Try to look at it that way."

She could hear her mother start to cry again. Wasn't that a silly thing to do? Hell, she was just going on a short trip. The farm wasn't very far away and her mother could visit her any time she wanted to come. It wasn't like Jack, going away for two years. It didn't amount to anything at all.

Her mother would find that out some day. They would all find it out. All this stupid talk and crying was for nothing. Della knew where she was going. It might take her a little time to get Roy into line, but it would be worth the effort because he had some money and he had a business and he was dumb. She was smart. She was smart enough to get it all.

Someone had hold of one of her hands, and the man with the deep voice was causing a lot of trouble by telling everybody about her trip. She wished that he'd stop talking about it. She didn't want anybody to know about where she was going, or what she was going to do, or anything at all. It was none of their business.

When she got back she'd let them know how she made out....

THE END

Orrie Hitt was born in Colchester, New York, on October 27, 1916. He married Charlotte Tucker in Port Jervis, New York, where they settled and had four children. Hitt wrote approximately 150 books over a period of about 14 years while sitting at his kitchen table surrounded by iced coffee, noisy children and Winston cigarettes. In his prime, he wrote a new novel every two weeks. Though

most of his books are now categorized as sleaze novels, Orrie Hitt perfectly captured the not-so-quiet desperation of the working class in the continual search for sex, money and happiness. He died in a VA hospital in Montrose, New York, from cancer on September 7, 1975.

Black Gat Books

Black Gat Books is a new line of mass market paperbacks introduced in 2015 by Stark House Press. New titles appear every three months, featuring the best in crime fiction reprints. Each book is sized to 4.25" x 7", just like they used to be. Collect them all!

Haven for the Damned by Harry Whittington
978-1-933586-75-5 $9.99

1 A group of eight people all converge on a small ghost town on the outskirts of the Mexican border, each with their own demons and dilemmas. They all want something they've lost: freedom, a lost wife, their youth. Not all of them will leave alive. May 2015.

Eddie's World by Charlie Stella
978-1-933586-76-2 $9.99

2 Charlie Stella's first great crime novel, back in print and available in paperback for the first time! Eddie Senta is suffering a mid-life crisis and decides to get involved in a heist. Everything that can go wrong, does. May 2015.

Stranger at Home by Leigh Brackett writing as George Sanders
978-1-933586-78-6 $9.99

3 Originally published as by the actor George Sanders, this domestic mystery by science fiction author Leigh Brackett is the story of a rich heel who comes back to get even with those who thought they had left him for dead. May 2015.

The Persian Cat by John Flagg
978-1933586-90-8 $9.99

4 A post-World War II thriller set in Teheran featuring cynical agent Gil Denby. His mission: bring a beautiful traitor to justice. His adversary: a major arms dealer. His odds: slim. August 2015.

Only the Wicked by Gary Phillips
978-1-933586-93-9 $9.99

5 The fourth Ivan Monk mystery, never before published in paperback. A tense Los Angeles thriller with roots in the Deep South. Author Sara Paretsky calls Phillips "my kind of crime writer and Ivan Monk is my kind of detective." November 2015.

Felony Tank by Malcolm Braly
978-1-933586-91-5 $9.99

6 Seventeen-year-old Doug is in the wrong place at the wrong time and ends up in jail. What happens next could only have been written by the author of *It's Cold Out There*. February 2016.

The Girl on the Bestseller List by Vin Packer
978-1-933586-98-4 $9.99

7 They all had a reason to hate Gloria Whealdon after she exposed their lives in her bestselling novel—but only one had a reason to kill. "I've read a number of Vin Packer's books, and this one remains a favorite." —*Bill Crider's Pop Culture Magazine*. May 2016.

She Got What She Wanted by Orrie Hitt
978-1-944520-04-5 $9.99

8 "This is a fine novel, sleaze paperback or literary, [on] how difficult it was for a woman not to have to resort to using her body and sexuality to get ahead in life." –Michael Hemmingson, *Those Sexy Vintage Sleaze Books*. August 2016.

The Woman on the Roof by Helen Nielsen
978-1-944520-13-7 $9.99

9 "Best whodunit of the year."—Springfield News and Leader. "Among the best mysteries of the year." —Mystery Writers of America. Black Gat #9. November 2016.

Stark House Press

1315 H Street, Eureka, CA 95501 707-498-3135
griffinskye3@sbcglobal.net www.starkhousepress.com
Available from your local bookstore or direct from the publisher.

* 9 7 8 1 9 4 4 5 2 0 0 4 5 *